The Dead Diva
A Sissy and Miss Boo Mystery

by

Nancy Smith Gibson

This book is fiction. All characters, events, and organizations portrayed in this novel are the product of the author's imagination or are used fictitiously. Any resemblance to actual persons—living or dead—is entirely coincidental.

Copyright © 2023 by Nancy Smith Gibson

All rights reserved. No parts of this book may be reproduced or transmitted in any form or by any means, electronic or mechanical, including photocopying, recording or by any information storage and retrieval system, without written permission from the author, except for the inclusion of brief quotations in a review.

For information, visit our website at:
www.cozycatpress.com

ISBN: 978-1-952579-62-2

Printed in the United States of America

10 9 8 7 6 5 4 3 2 1

This book is dedicated to Lin Fewell, a friend and fellow church member of Christway Unity Church. Thank you for allowing me to use your name for one of my characters. Happy 100th Birthday!

CHAPTER ONE

Aunt Lola always says, "Karma will bite them in the ass," when she hears about somebody doing something bad and getting away with it. "You watch," she says. "Karma will catch up to them." She believes that if you are good—and by that she means honest, fair, and kind—Karma will reward you, but if you are bad, paybacks will land on you as well, but they won't be good ones. Not good at all.

When my fiancé, Bobby Ray Shoemaker, jilted me, practically at the altar, and ran off to marry Rita Combs, I wondered what I had done to deserve the embarrassment and heartache that visited itself on me, but Aunt Lola said it wasn't me who did wrong. No sir. It was karma letting me escape from a marriage to some low-life cheater like Bobby Ray. "Think about it," she said. "What if you'd married him and had a couple of kids, and *then* he ran off with another woman? Wouldn't that have been worse?" And I had to admit she was right. It would have been, but for a while it was hard to see that side of the matter.

I also had to admit that she was right when she told me life would be better without him. "Just wait and see," she told me as she handed me another box of tissues. "Tell me in six months or so if I'm not right. This wouldn't have happened if something better wasn't going to come along."

And she was spot on. Things started looking up when I took all my wedding money, bought myself a baby-blue convertible, and took off for the coast—the Mississippi gulf coast, that is—intending to get a job down there and start over. I started a new life all right, it just wasn't the life I had first planned. And it was going as smooth as . . . well, I guess I might not say that it was as smooth as a baby's butt—that didn't sound appropriate—but it was smooth all right.

Along the way to my new life, I gave a ride to a nice, little old lady—Miss Boo—who was also going to the gulf coast. We rescued an abandoned dog, found a dead body, were almost arrested for murder, and . . . well, all sorts of things happened, but I ended up in a much better spot than I'd been in back in Pecan Grove. Now I'm living in Miss Boo's garage apartment, working as a receptionist-slash reporter for the *Mount Chapel News*, and I have not one but *two* almost boyfriends. I probably could promote either one of them from almost to full boyfriend status if I was willing to give up the other one. But I'm not. Not willing. Not going to. I don't think.

Porter Quinn is the official photographer for the *Mount Chapel News*, which is the weekly paper that everyone in town reads. He's cute and sweet and takes me to the movies and out to nice restaurants for dinner. He's polite, kind, and holds doors open for me and is just the type of person my parents would want their daughter to date. Who would give up someone like that?

Asher Donovan is Miss Boo's grandson. He's a detective for the Mount Chapel Police Department. He spends a lot of time working undercover, and when he's incognito, he doesn't shave, wears tattoo sleeves, and rides a motorcycle. No matter how he's dressed, he's a good kisser. Better than good. Sizzling. In front of his grandmother, he's polite and kind. Otherwise, he's sending dagger-like glances at me while I'm trying to decipher the meaning behind them. If he's wearing his bad boy disguise, my mother would have a heart attack knowing I was even in the same room with Ash Donovan, much less kissing him.

So maybe I can't figure out the details of the karma aspect as it deals with Asher and Porter, but it's not hard to figure out as it relates to Lorraine Coggins, aka LaRue Saint Pierre.

CHAPTER TWO

"Sissy, Mr. Hoskins would like to speak with you as soon as you have time," the boss's secretary, Mrs. Frewer, said as she gathered the papers from his "in" box. She frowned as she said it, which worried me a bit. I couldn't think of anything I'd done to produce that expression, since she usually smiles at me when she ventures as far away from her desk as the reception area in the front of the *Mount Chapel News* office, which wasn't often. She usually summons me by way of the telephone, so for her to come all the way up front is unusual. She could have said, "Bring the mail when you come," but she didn't. Something was up, and I didn't have a clue as to what it might be.

"I'll be right there, Mrs. F.," I responded. The phone rang, and I had to answer a couple of questions, then I gathered a stenographer's notebook and a pen and started toward Mr. Hoskins's office. I didn't know if I would need to make notes, but just holding the tools to do so made me feel more professional—like I had a purpose and I knew what it is.

"Go right on in, Sissy. He's expecting you," she said when I reached the desk where she guards the privacy of the inner sanctum.

"Come on in, Sissy. Have a seat," the man behind the desk said, waving me into his office. Gene Hoskins is the head honcho at the *Mount Chapel News*, but he's as friendly and easy to talk to as any of the people working in the big, open room that serves as an office to the reporters, department heads, and clerks who work at the paper. This time he seemed nervous, which was unusual for him. He didn't look directly at me as he leaned back in his office chair, rubbing his hand over the top of his head. I wondered if that was how it got so bald on top, with him rubbing it when he was worried about something.

"How are you doing?" he asked. "How is Boo?"

"I'm fine. Miss Boo is fine." *Surely he didn't bring me in here to ask about my health or anyone else's,* I mused. He always asked about my friend and landlady, Emily "Boo" Bryce. Of course, that could be because Miss Boo is one of the richest and most influential people in town. Could be. But I personally thought it was because he had the hots for her—if people their age still get the hots for anyone. When Miss Boo comes by to meet me for lunch, Gene Hoskins always manages to show up at my desk and wrangle his way into the conversation. Sometimes he ends up going to eat with us. I also think Miss Boo might come by so Mr. Hoskins will do just that. I mean, Miss Boo is my friend and all, but why would she come by my workplace just to go to lunch with me?

"Sissy, you've been doing just fine writing those little columns you came up with," he said. He smiled. "Just fine," he repeated, like he was stuck on the word 'fine'.

"I enjoy writing them, Mr. Hoskins, both the weekly library column and the "Getting to Know the Local Businesses" articles, too." *Maybe he has an idea for another local feature for me to write, but why would that make him so nervous?*

"Maybe you're ready for a little bigger assignment." He picked up a paper clip and started bending it this way and that.

"Yes, sir," I said. Maybe he was smiling because he was happy with me, but I doubted it. I still thought there was something odd going on.

"Did you know we have a famous author living here in Mount Chapel? LaRue Saint Pierre bought an estate—the old Briarwood place—and has moved to town."

"I've heard that," I said. "I don't read romance novels much, but I know who she is. People are talking about her moving to town and all. She's been having a lot of work done on the house and grounds, I hear."

"Yes, everybody's heard of LaRue Saint Pierre. One or another of her books is always on the Best Seller list, and they're going to make one of them into a movie," he said. He concentrated on bending the piece of wire in his hand. He frowned. "And she wants to give an interview to the *Mount Chapel News*. An exclusive."

"Oh? That's great." *That sounds like something good to me, so why is he frowning? Why won't he look at me?*

"She's refurbishing the flower garden at Briarwood, and word around town is that she's going to change the name of the place to Daisywood. I understand her books are put into categories according to what kind of . . . uh—heat level, I think they call it—suits it. Like a pink daisy for a book with no . . . um. . ." He couldn't go any further with that thought, not out loud anyway. "A red daisy for more explicit. . ." He almost blushed as he tried to explain. "And so on. And she's going to have flowers named after her books."

"That sounds interesting." *Maybe it did if you like her books and flowers.*

"Do you think you can handle that, Sissy?" he suddenly asked.

My mind must have wandered as he talked because I had lost the train of what he was saying. "Me?" I asked.

"You. Sissy Townley. Do you think you could handle interviewing her?" He changed from looking at the paper clip in his hands to looking at me. He was still frowning.

"But . . ." I had never interviewed anyone famous, or even semi-famous. I could ask the head librarian questions. *What books are most popular these days, Mrs. Burroughs?* Or even the owner of the furniture store. *What would you say is the go-to color for living room furniture this season?* But a best-selling author? This might be a challenge. "Wouldn't that be more to Marilee's, er, talent?"

Marilee Hubbard is the society editor for the *News*, and she defends her right to any and all stories that even vaguely came under the umbrella of 'society'. I felt quite sure she would fight for a story concerning a world-famous author living right here in Mount Chapel. It might be the end of my so-called career to take a story right from under Marilee's nose, even if Gene Hoskins assigned it to me.

"It's like this, Sissy. Marilee went to visit her sister in Georgia, and as she was preparing to come back home, she fell coming down some steps and broke her leg. She's in the hospital in Savannah. She had an appointment with Miss Saint Pierre for tomorrow morning. We tried to change it—put it off a couple of weeks—but Miss Saint Pierre wouldn't hear of it. Either show up tomorrow morning at ten o'clock or forget the interview." He looked at me with puppy-dog eyes. "I don't want us to lose this. It might even go national."

"And you trust me to do it?"

"Sure," he said in a hearty tone. His voice dropped just a bit as he admitted the truth of the matter. "I don't have anyone else I can send. A man just wouldn't do to interview a romance writer. We just don't get it the way you women do. A man wouldn't even know what questions to ask."

"*I* don't even know what questions to ask!"

"I have faith in you, Sissy. You can start thinking now about what the women who read LaRue St. Pierre's books want to know. About her and about the books that have made her famous. Who knows, this interview might make *you* famous."

"I guess," I said dubiously.

"Why don't you take the rest of the day off," he said as he leaned forward and took his wallet from his hip pocket. "Go buy a couple of her books. The Book Nook is bound to have them, what with her being so popular and living here in Mount Chapel and all. Maybe you can skim through them and come up with some questions to ask about how she came up with the ideas." He handed me some bills. "Don't come in to work tomorrow before you interview Miss Saint Pierre. You can tell me then how it goes . . . er . . . went."

I went by my desk to get my purse, then left on my special assignment. This would either be a feather in my cap, as my father would say, or my downfall. I took a deep breath and hoped for the best.

CHAPTER THREE

The Book Nook carried LaRue Saint Pierre's books—all twenty titles. A table in the front of the store had stacks of them, along with a big picture of the author. Her face looked serious, sultry even, as if the photographer had caught her in the throes of passion. Ethereal like the swath of fabric that draped around her, she was not as sexy as the models on the fronts of the books, still, she could have posed for most of the pictures. It wasn't until much later that I figured out that the pictures of the author were deliberately shot that way in order to disguise the fact that she was decades older than the women she portrayed in her books. The models and the author had lots of blonde hair, tangled in wild profusion, as if the handsome man who stared passionately at the woman in his arms had been running his fingers through her tresses for the last few hours. LaRue Saint Pierre's poster didn't have a man beside her, but it looked like she was thinking about one.

"May I help you?" A clerk appeared as I stood looking at the display.

"I was just trying to decide which one to buy," I said.

"They're all just wonderful," she said, running her fingers over the nearest offering, *Mistress of Passion*. The stack of novels next to it was *Passion Driven*, and the next was *Bound by Passion*. "These are all the Passion series on this end of the table. Which ones have you read?"

"Er . . . actually, I haven't read any of them," I admitted.

"Oh," she said, sounding surprised. "Well, all the Passion series have a little, red daisy in the corner. See?" She pointed out the deep, red flower on the cover. "They're all very . . . um . . . descriptive."

"Descriptive?" Something in me wanted to make her say it.

"You know. The love scenes. They're descriptive."

"The sex scenes, you mean?"

"Yes, the . . . ah . . . sex scenes."

"What if I don't want to read anything that graphic?"

"Well, then you'd look for a pink daisy on the cover. See?" She moved around to the other side of the table and picked up another book. The couple on the cover looked at each other admiringly, but on this particular book, the woman's boobs were completely covered, unlike the red daisy books, and she and the man were simply smiling at each other. Also, unlike the red daisy books, they didn't look like they were about to jump each other's bones.

"I see some have a yellow daisy on them. What's that mean?"

"Those have older couples falling in love. Like widows and divorcees."

"Older?"

"Thirties and forties. Maybe even older. I haven't read any of those," she said.

"Which ones are the most popular?" I might as well start with the ones most readers were interested in.

"Well, the Passion books are pretty popular, but I think we sell more of the *Chateau* series than anything." She patted a stack of books, each with a picture of a barely dressed woman. A man stood behind her, his arms enfolding her just under her ample . . . er . . . bosom. In the background was a castle. The title was *Chateau L'Amour. Castle of Love.* There were two more stacks adjacent, *Chateau d'Temptation,* and *Chateau d'Desire.* They all had a red flower on the corner. I didn't think that was the way to use a d' on a word, but who am I to judge? She's the successful novelist; I'm just a small-town reporter.

I thanked her for helping me, and after studying the back cover of several, I ended up buying one of each color flower. I doubted that I'd be able to read all three before tomorrow's interview, but maybe I could get through enough to pose intelligent questions. This was the oddest research I could imagine doing for a story. Maybe being a reporter/receptionist was going to be more interesting than I'd previously thought.

When I got home, I fixed myself a cola to sip and settled myself on my comfortable couch, lamp at my shoulder, pillow propping up my elbow, ready to spend the day reading and thinking up questions to ask Miss Saint Pierre. I started with the pink daisy book. It didn't catch my interest much, all concerned with looks and sighs and how handsome the hero was and how the heroine ached and yearned to feel his manly arms around her. I skipped a lot and moved on to the red daisy book.

I wouldn't have thought that sex could be boring, but there are just so many heaving bosoms and rigid . . . well, *body parts . . .* you can read about without wanting to yell, "Why don't you get out of bed (or off the floor or out of the hay loft) and go do something else?" I mean, I like sex as much as the next person, but come on! Enough is enough, already!

At noon I got up and fixed myself a peanut butter sandwich and tried to read more passion, passion, passion as I ate. Giving up on canoodling among red daisies, I moved on to the yellow flower book. That lasted awhile, as the recently widowed mother of a little boy got a job working for a demanding, good-looking (of course) divorced businessman caught my attention for the first couple of chapters. But the couch was comfortable, and I slid down, wiggled my way into its plushy depths, and drifted off to sleep.

I woke when my phone, conveniently placed on the end table in case the office needed to call me for anything, woke me. Yeah, right! Like I'm so important at the *Mount Chapel News* that someone might have to call me.

"Sissy? Is everything all right?" Miss Boo sounded worried. "Your car was there when I left late this morning, and it's still there. Are you sick?"

I sat up and rubbed my face with my hand, trying to figure out what I was doing on my sofa in the middle of the day, instead of at the office. "No, Miss Boo. I'm okay. Mr. Hoskins has me doing research for an assignment he gave me. I've been reading all day, but I fell sleep."

"That sounds promising. Gene gave you a special assignment, did he?"

"Yes, an interview. I'm doing it tomorrow morning, and I was trying to get prepared for it. Think up questions to ask and all that."

"Sissy, I'm getting ready to pop a casserole into the oven, and I'm making a salad. Why don't you come over for supper? Doris is coming and bringing desert. We'd love to hear about who you're going to interview."

Doris Benton is Miss Boo's BFF. They went to school together back in the day, and they have dinner together a couple of times a month to catch up on town gossip and share good food. With a special dinner planned, there was a possibility that Miss Boo's grandson, Asher, might be coming too. He sometimes showed up unannounced to take advantage of his grandmother's kitchen, although she seldom cooked any longer, preferring to get the pre-assembled dishes offered by the local deli. Miss Boo and Doris considered it a good way to find out what was going on about town, with the local detective and undercover agent trading information for food.

"Give me time to freshen up, Miss Boo, and I'll be there." I wasn't going to pass up a chance for a meal that I didn't have to cook, especially if super sexy cop Ash Donovan might be there.

CHAPTER FOUR

It took me about thirty minutes to shower, put on a cute sundress that showed a bit of bare skin, use a curling iron on my shoulder length hair, and apply some light makeup. Just in case, you know, Asher dropped by his grandmother's kitchen at suppertime, unannounced.

"You're just in time," Miss Boo said when I slipped in her back door. Larry greeted me with a wagging tail and sniffed my feet to see if I'd been anyplace interesting. Not smelling any other dog scents around me, he went back to his bed with a sigh.

"I'm glad you could come over," Doris Benton said. "I haven't had a chance to visit with you lately. Has anything thrilling happened to you? Any FBI agents in disguise? Bodies in the bushes? Dogs with clues on microchips?"

"Not a thing, Mrs. Benton. Life has been pretty calm." Ever since Miss Boo and I had found that dead body, people kept thinking that we have exciting things occurring in our lives all the time.

"Please call me Doris," Mrs. Benton said. "Mrs. Benton is just too formal, and I don't have a nickname like Boo does."

"Everything's ready," Miss Boo said as she put a couple of bottles of salad dressing on the kitchen table alongside the bowl of salad and slid a basket of garlic bread onto the table next to the steaming casserole dish. "Let's eat."

We sat down at the big, round oak table, prettily set with green place mats and gaily decorated dishes. After Miss Boo said a brief blessing, we started dishing up the casserole and the salad made of all sorts of vegetables. My stomach was telling me that I'd only had a PB&J for lunch and it was ready for more.

"So, Sissy, tell us about this interview you're going to do. Gene must think you have real potential as a reporter to send you instead of one of the other news people who work at the *News,*" Miss Boo said.

"To tell the truth, he was kind of in a bind. Marilee Hubbard was supposed to do it, but she was visiting her daughter in Savannah when she fell and broke her leg. She's still in the hospital there, and the appointment can't be rescheduled, so I'm doing it."

"Bad luck for Marilee. Good luck for you. Who's it with?" Doris asked as she forked up a bite of chicken and pasta.

"It's with a famous author who's moved to Mount Chapel," I answered, pouring some ranch dressing over a sizeable serving of salad. "Have you ever heard of LaRue Saint Pierre?"

I had heard the expression "the silence was deafening" before, but I'd never thought about what it really meant. I looked up as I screwed the lid back on the bottle. Both Doris and Miss Boo were staring at me, forks in midair with food dangling.

"Huh!" Doris muttered. She looked at Miss Boo.

"I heard she was back in town," Miss Boo said to Doris.

"Bought that big old house—the one the bootleggers used back in the '20s. What do they call it?"

"Briarwood," Miss Boo answered. "She always did have to have the biggest . . ." She stopped talking and ate the bite of casserole on her fork.

"Yes, I remember when she had that surgery. Went from 36B to 42 double D in one step. Always the biggest," Doris said, and she snickered, as did Miss Boo.

"You know Miss Saint Pierre?" I asked.

"We knew her before she was LaRue Saint Pierre," Miss Boo said.

"Before she was a double D," Doris added.

"We knew her when she was plain ol' Lorraine Coggins." Miss Boo sniffed. "She was our friend's little sister."

"I was wondering why she picked Mount Chapel to move to," I said. "I mean, it's a nice town and all, but an unusual place for a New York City best-selling author to move to."

"To show off," Doris said.

"To say 'I told you so'," Miss Boo said.

"To prove to all the folks who'd said she'd never amount to anything that they were wrong." Doris Benton poked at her pasta with her fork.

"Well, they were," Miss Boo said. "She did turn out to be somebody—but I wonder what, exactly, she's like these days. If she's any nicer or happier than she was when she was Lily Coggins's little sister."

"Do you really think she might be?" Doris questioned her friend.

"Some people do change, Doris," Miss Boo said. "They grow up and wise up when life hands them lessons." She took a sip of iced tea. "So, you're going to meet her, Sissy? Write a story about her?"

"Yessum. Mr. Robinson had me go buy some of her books. That's what I was doing home today—reading. I have to come up with some questions to ask her."

"Ask her why she moved back to Mount Chapel," Doris said, looking at me over the top of her glasses.

"You've said why," Miss Boo said. "To show off her fame to all us poor, unfamous people."

"She won't say that, though," Doris said. "She'll have some fancy answer. I'd like to know what she's claiming is the reason."

"Well, it's not that she's slinking home, broke." Miss Boo served herself another scoop of chicken and pasta. "She paid a pretty penny for that house she bought, and she's redoing the grounds."

"She'll probably have garden tours when she has it finished."

"I'm never going to pay even one dollar to see Lorraine Coggins's home or garden." Miss Boo sniffed. "She was always so ugly to everyone, especially her mother and grandmother. She treated Lily like she was dirt, even when Lily tried to help her. I'm not going to act like she's some role model we ought to look up to just because she writes dirty books." She placed her napkin beside her plate, and ignoring the food she'd just served herself, she pushed back from the table. "Anyone ready for dessert? Doris, your strawberry trifle looks wonderful."

As Miss Boo dished up the strawberry-soaked cake into fancy, green, stemmed dishes, Doris turned to me. "Are they, Sissy? Dirty books? I've never read one. I just couldn't bring myself to walk into the Book Nook and buy one. Not with what everyone was saying about them."

"Well, they are pretty . . . steamy," I said, contemplating the words to describe them. "You know there are three different . . . categories."

"What do you mean?"

"Red daisy books are very . . . explicit."

"Explicit?"

Miss Boo sat back down at the table. "They talk about sex, Doris. Use words neither of us have probably ever heard spoken aloud. Words I don't want to read."

"Yes," I agreed. "But you might like her pink daisy books. They aren't so . . ."

"Spicy?" Miss Boo said as I stumbled for a word.

"Yes. Not so spicy. They wouldn't embarrass you to read. They are usually about teenagers or what people call 'young adults.'"

"No sex?" Doris asked.

"Oh, there might be sex, but she doesn't spell it out. It happens behind closed doors, as the expression goes."

"Red or pink daisies, huh?" Doris thought about it as she took a bite of strawberries covered in whipped cream.

"Or yellow," I said.

"What's yellow for?" Doris asked.

"What she calls love stories with older characters."

"What do you mean by older?" Miss Boo asked.

"I only bought one of those, and I fell sleep before I got too far into it, but I think that means maybe forty or fifty-ish."

Both Miss Boo and Doris chuckled. "Honey, at that age you're just getting started," Doris said.

"We know how old Lorraine Coggins is," Miss Boo said. "She ought to be writing about lovers in their sixties or seventies."

"There wouldn't be much to write about, Boo," Doris said.

"Speak for yourself, Doris. Speak for yourself."

CHAPTER FIVE

I helped with cleanup, then went back to my apartment over the garage. Miss Boo's grandson hadn't shown up for dinner, but I had gained something almost as good as seeing and bantering with the sexy policeman. Background information about the famous author living right here in Mount Chapel. I wouldn't put something like that out for everyone and their brother to read, but who knows? It might come to be valuable at some point, knowing that LaRue Saint Pierre, presumably from New York City and Paris, France, was born Lorraine Coggins of Mount Chapel, Mississippi. Maybe I could ask some questions about what it was like to move back to the town where she had grown up.

I jotted a few questions in my stenographer's notebook and put it beside my bed, just in case I woke up and thought of something else in the middle of the night. The next morning, I hadn't added anything, but as I ate breakfast and dressed, several queries came to mind:

Which of the books you've written is your favorite?

Do you get any of your ideas from real people or real situations?

Do you write with paper and pen? Or on the computer? Or typewriter?

Do you need isolation to write? Or are you like the famous author who sits in a café or coffee shop to work?

How long does it take you to write a book?

I finished eating and rinsed my cereal bowl and juice glass, leaving them on the rubber mat to drain.

The next problem was what to wear. I had come to the conclusion a few months ago that my choices in clothing ought to reflect a stylish woman, not a fun-loving teenager. After all, I'd been in my twenties for a couple of years now, while my wardrobe still pegged me as a high-school student.

If I wanted people to take me seriously, maybe I needed to look the part. Pinterest gave me ideas and guidance, and I had gradually been adding pieces that made me look more grown up. I'd save my jeans and tees for home.

But what do you wear to interview a *New York Times* Best-Selling Author? After several changes, I ended up in a dress—kind of short, but not *too* short, if you know what I mean. Not so short that my mama would say, "Lord, child, you can see France in that outfit. Go change clothes." I added a black suit jacket that made me look quite professional. I started to slip into my highest heels to set the whole thing off but decided that eff-me shoes were not called for, so I settled for more lady-like, but stylish, black pumps. Along with a purse big enough to hold a small tape recorder and my handy-dandy notebook and pen, I was dressed and ready to tackle the interview. *Sissy Townley, girl reporter, on the job,* I thought as I looked into the full-length mirror on the closet door. *Correction! Cecelia Townley, woman reporter.* I nodded to myself before I turned to leave.

***

Briarwood is on the east side of Mount Chapel. When it was originally built, it was out in the country, sitting on several hundred acres, more or less, of prime cotton-growing land. At least that's what Doris and Miss Boo told me last night. The house that stood now replaced the old ante bellum mansion that had been there until fire destroyed it around the turn of the twentieth century. Land had been sold off until all that remained of the original plantation was about five acres and a large red brick home, built during the prohibition era. It had been remodeled from generation to generation and was now surrounded by upscale houses built in the last twenty years or so. Over time, a lawyer had lived in the house that stood there now, and a doctor, and others, I assume. They had all kept the old name, the one the cotton plantation had gone by. It was Briarwood a hundred and fifty years ago, and it was still Briarwood today. Lorraine Coggins, aka LaRue Saint Pierre, had had the place redecorated to her taste before she ever moved in. I wondered if Miss Saint Pierre would allow the *Mount Chapel News* to do a photo shoot of the interior of the house. Maybe I could work that into the conversation.

I had a pretty good list of questions to ask—enough to make an interesting article. I wondered if she wanted it known that she used to live in Mount Chapel as a child and young adult, or if that was supposed to be kept secret. I'd have to work that question into the interview in some way as well.

When I arrived, I pulled my car off the street onto the beginning of the drive up to the house. The whole place was surrounded by red brick posts holding sections of black wrought iron fencing. This was a recent addition. I guess a famous author needs a barrier to keep fans off her private property, while ordinary people—doctors and lawyers and such—didn't have to worry about that. There was a metal box built into the massive brick column on the left side of the drive. It had the word 'phone' etched on it. Even I, unsophisticated as I am, knew that if visitors opened the little door, they would find a telephone inside. Somebody in the house would answer, and if you were to be admitted, they would push a button to open the massive iron gate so you could drive up to the house. I knew how it worked because I'd seen it in movies and television, protecting movie stars, rich people, or mobsters from the public. I never imagined seeing it in a small Mississippi town.

But the gate stood wide open. Maybe Lorraine wasn't having the problem of unwanted visitors that she thought she would. Or maybe, since she was expecting Marilee Hubbard, it was left open to welcome her guest.

I drove up the lane to the house, where a loop of drive circled a statue of a semi-nude woman, draped in stone fabric that covered her private parts. The jar in her arms spilled a continuous stream of water into the pool at her feet. Maybe I could arrange for Porter Quinn, the official photographer for the *News* and my sort of boyfriend, to come take a picture of it. The garden clubs in town—and Mount Chapel had several—would love to see it. Heck, most everybody in the county would like to see it. And when they did, I'll bet everyone would just have to have one in their own yard. Until they heard the price tag attached. Fancy statues and ponds and recirculating water can't come cheap, but they could probably find a cheaper version at one of those roadside places that sell concrete birdbaths and such. Before long, there'll probably be statues in front yards all over town, but the ones that spill water all the time might be harder to come by.

I parked and approached the front door with some edginess. This was my first important interview, and how well I did on this assignment would determine if Gene Hoskins let me do any more. I had my list of questions to ask, and I was as organized as I could be after having only one day to study. I hoped she wouldn't ask me any questions about her books. Like how many I had read, or which one I liked best. I couldn't do more at this point, so I took a deep breath and pushed the doorbell. Inside, I heard the chiming tones announcing my arrival.

I waited what I thought was sufficient time and punched the button again. The sound was loud in the morning air. Too loud. I looked at the massive door blocking unwelcome intruders from just walking in. It was open by several inches. In my nervousness, I hadn't noticed until the volume of the door chime brought it to my attention.

With one finger, I pushed the door open wider. Not too wide, just enough so that I could see the foyer. A marble floor gleamed underfoot, and in the center was an overelaborate table on which there was a vase of red roses. Naked cherubs appeared to be holding the bouquet. Miss Saint Pierre evidently had a thing for almost naked people, both on her books and in her home. Further along the entrance hall, wide marble steps rose to the second floor.

I took one step inside the threshold and called out, "Miss Saint Pierre? Hello?" and listened for an answer. Surely she was expecting me. Well . . . not me, exactly, but I understood that she set up the interview herself, so she was expecting Marilee Hubbard. Or somebody. She ought to be here. Maybe she had to go to the bathroom at the last minute. That happened to me sometimes. All ready to go, and then I had to go.

I called out again. "Miss Saint Pierre? Cecelia Townley here. From the *Mount Chapel News*." I stood still and listened but didn't hear anything. "I'm here to do your interview." No voice called back to me. No footsteps signaled someone was coming. I took a couple of steps more and looked around. To the left, an elegantly decorated dining room adjoined the front hall, and I took a few steps inside the elegant room. A long mahogany table ran down the center of the space, surrounded by a lot of chairs. I didn't count them, but I imagine a dozen people, maybe more, could be seated for dinner. On the far wall there was an oil painting of a reclining nude woman. The subject looked like a blonde who might grace the cover of one of LaRue Saint Pierre's red daisy books. There was a drape of cloth on the figures, both the ones on the novels and the one on the wall, but it didn't cover enough, in my opinion, in either case. Again, I wondered if the author had also been the artist's model. Surely not. Who would want a painting of their naked self on the wall of their dining room? Maybe Lorraine did. The question tumbled through my mind as I stood there, but I didn't think I had the nerve to ask Miss Saint Pierre if she had posed for the painting or the book covers.

I withdrew to the foyer and called out again, with the same results. That is to say, nothing. It was obvious I was going to have to do something, but what? In front of me was the wide staircase leading to the upper floor. To the right was the uh . . . parlor? Living room? What did one call the space in such a fancy house? It didn't look like anyone could do much living in it. Personally, I'd be afraid I'd mess something up. Put a footprint in the deep carpet. Move a sofa pillow out of place. I eased into the pristine room.

As I stood in the middle of the room, I called out once more, "Miss Saint Pierre? Hello? I'm here from the *Mount Chapel News* for your interview." It might have been my imagination, but I thought I heard the merest hint of a sound coming from somewhere in the depths of the house. There was a door on the back wall, and I went to it. Rapping lightly, I said her name once more as I opened the door to what was obviously a library, or maybe an office.

Bookcases lined the back wall. A large desk commanded the room, and a lamp focused its light on the papers scattered about, suggesting that somebody had recently been working there. Several comfortable-looking leather chairs offered seating.

I advanced farther into the room, and when I reached the side of the desk, I saw her. It. I saw the dead body.

CHAPTER SIX

I sat down on the front steps to wait for the police. It was too spooky to wait in the house with the body of the person I'd been supposed to interview spread out on the floor, covered in blood.

I'll admit that I had stayed in there long enough to look around just a bit. LaRue Saint Pierre's body was behind the big mahogany desk. It looked as if she'd been sitting in the chair, pushed back, stood up, and was shot standing there. She'd left a trail of blood on the brown leather as she sunk to the floor. A mass of blonde hair obscured most of her face, like maybe her wig had slipped. Tiny wrinkles spread out from her bright red lips, contradicting the appearance of youth she was trying for. The low-cut white dress she had donned—probably in anticipation of impressing the reporter who was coming to write her success story—was now stained with her blood, red and wet. Not that I touched it, but it looked as if it hadn't been there long.

My heart nearly jumped out of my chest when I spotted the body, but I took a deep breath and regained my composure. Whipping out my cell phone, I started taking pictures of everything—the body, the desk, and all of the surrounding area. Papers lay all about, some partially under the body. I leaned close and got shots of those, along with the ones still on the desk.

Looking around the office, I saw nothing else out of the ordinary: comfortable chairs for guests and bookcases covering the back wall. They appeared to hold all of LaRue Saint Pierre's novels plus others. Framed book covers were displayed on the walls, with the sultry cover models sending sexy looks at bare-chested heroes. Was this the room where I would have conducted the interview? If the morning had gone as planned, I would be sitting in one of those chairs asking my questions. But the morning had gone anything but planned.

At this point, the creepiness of the situation began to sink in. I was all alone in a big house with a dead body, and the murderer might well be lurking somewhere close by. I like the word 'lurking'. It's full of suspense and dread, which is good in a novel, but not so much in person. It settled on me like a veil, so I got myself out of that room and out of that house quickly, before whoever shot Lorraine decided to shoot me as well. I didn't have any reason to think they would, but when you're spooked, you don't need a reason. That creepy feeling can take over at any time and there's nothing you can do about it.

I scurried through the parlor, hurrying as best as I could with the deep pile carpet holding onto my feet as if I were plowing through molasses. As quickly as my suddenly weak legs could carry me, I passed through the vestibule and out the front door. I got as far as my car before I stopped. Leaning against the baby-blue convertible that was my pride and joy, I placed my hands on the still warm hood and drew on it for strength. It was a beautiful day and nobody was after me. I was alive and unharmed, at least so far. I had survived other misfortunes far worse than finding a dead body, such as my disastrous engagement to Bobby Joe. I had come out on the other side of that fiasco in better shape than I would ever have imagined. Here I stood, counting my blessings, with a kick-ass car, an interesting job, two sort-of boyfriends, and . . . a story to write. A story that everybody would want to read. One that was, at this point, an exclusive. One might say it was a good day . . . for me. For Lorraine Coggins, aka LaRue Saint Pierre, not so much.

I took a deep breath and looked back at the house, the front door standing wide open. I was alone and nobody was coming after me. I had panicked for no good reason. *Think, Sissy! Think!* My phone was still in my hand from taking pictures of the murder scene. I punched 911 and waited.

Explaining to the police operator wasn't easy. She couldn't seem to understand what I was doing in the home of someone I'd never met and how I'd found a dead body and why I was so sure she was dead. And since I didn't know her, why was I so sure that it was famous personage LaRue Saint Pierre?

Too many hows and whys that I couldn't answer. "Just come," I said. "No, you don't need an ambulance. It's too late for that. Yes, I'm sure. Because dead is dead."

I settled on the brick steps leading to the front door to wait. My mind jumped back to the other time I'd found a dead body. That time it had been in some bushes outside a casino. Miss Boo had been a calming influence at the time. She had known what to do and what to say, and if anyone knew how to talk to the police, it was Miss Boo. The local force was practically family to her, what with her grandson, Asher, being a detective there. I had her number on speed-dial.

"Miss Boo, you're never going to believe what has happened."

When I'd explained how I came to find the body, she asked, "Sissy, do you want me to come? Or would you rather I stay away?"

"I wish you'd come, Miss Boo. I'd feel better if you were here with me."

"I was hoping you'd say that," she said and hung up.

I had hardly taken the phone from my ear when a police car raced up the drive and pulled in behind my vehicle. The uniformed officer who got out hurried toward me. "Did you call in?" he asked, and I nodded.

"Where's . . ." he started.

I waved in the direction of the front door. "To the right. The room behind the living room." I saw no reason to see the murder scene again. The thought of all that blood was beginning to have an effect on my stomach.

He bounded up the steps, but paused before entering. "Stay right where you are," he said as an afterthought. "Don't go anywhere." He pointed his finger at me as he said it, like doing that would make me mind him. I mean, of course I was going to stay put, but if I wasn't, his shaking his finger wouldn't keep me from leaving if that was what I was going to do. And if I was going to leave, I would have already done it, instead of waiting around for the police.

"I wasn't planning on it," I said as he disappeared into the house. Miss Boo must have broken the speed limit getting from her house to Briarwood, because it only seemed like a couple of minutes before she arrived.

She parked behind the police cruiser and hurried to me. "Are you okay, Sissy?" she asked, sitting down beside me on the step.

"I think so," I answered. "It's beginning to sink in a bit. All that blood. . ."

The cop came out of the front door. "Miss Boo?" he said. "What are you doing here?"

"Hello, Walter," she answered. "Sissy is my friend, and I thought she needed someone with her at a time like this." She looked at me sympathetically. "Are you still feeling faint, Sissy?" she asked solicitously. "Maybe we need to get you something to drink. A shock like this can make your blood sugar dip. Don't you pass out now!"

She held my hand in one of hers while she rubbed my arm with the other one, and she eyed me, frowning, while doing so. I got the signal . . . *play along.*

"Walter, I think we need to get her inside, maybe on a couch so if she faints, she'll be on something soft. Come help me."

She put one hand under my elbow and heaved me upright. Still grasping my left hand, she guided me up the steps. Walter had no other choice but to come help Miss Boo get her patient into the house, which was where my benefactor wanted to be—where the action was. She gave me a little shove, just enough to put me off balance, and when I stumbled, she said, "Hold on, Sissy! Hold on!"

With Miss Boo on one side and Walter on the other, we progressed to the ornate, cherub-laden, pink and ivory living room. After glancing around, she guided me toward the velvet sofa, where she deposited me among the numerous pillows. Positioned so that anyone sitting there could see what was going on in that room, the vestibule, and the dining room across the way, it was the ideal post to observe the activity. The door into the office where I'd found the body was to our right. We could see everyone coming and going and hear most of the conversations.

As Miss Boo situated pillows behind my head, patted my hand, and murmured things like, "It's going to be okay, Sissy. Just close your eyes for a few minutes." We heard another car roar up the drive, and Walter left to go see who had arrived. Miss Boo used the opportunity to quickly look at the deceased then return to my side before the young officer returned. With the front door standing open, we could hear the conversation as the newcomer came up the steps.

"In the office," Walter said. "Appears to be shot."

"How long ago?" the new voice asked.

"Not long," Walter replied.

As they walked into the room, Miss Boo grasped my hand again, looked at me, and nodded toward the pillow behind my head. I leaned back and closed my eyes. I knew my cues.

"Chief McCray," Miss Boo said.

"Miss Boo," he replied. "What are you doing here?"

"My young friend here discovered the body."

"She did, did she? How did that come about?"

"She's a reporter for the *Mount Chapel News*, and she had an appointment to interview Miss Saint Pierre."

"And can she tell me that herself?"

"She can," Miss Boo replied as she gave my hand a squeeze. "She's just feeling a bit faint. The shock, you know." She reached up a smoothed a strand of imaginary hair off my face. In other words, stay quiet for now. "I'm going to get her a glass of water to help her revive herself. I'm sure she'll be ready for your questions in a few minutes."

"Don't touch anything, Miss Boo. Not anything," he cautioned.

"I know," she agreed. "I won't move anything. I won't leave my fingerprints anywhere. I know the drill." She stood up and went in the direction of the vestibule. Looking all around as if she were searching for a source of water for me, she went out of sight toward the rear of the house.

I heard him sniff, and he growled under his breath as he went toward the office door. I opened my eyes a bare slit and saw the portly officer follow Walter to the scene of the crime.

They kept their voices low, and try as I might, I couldn't make out much of what was being said in the next room. When they walked back into the parlor, my eyes were still closed, and I continued to rest on the pillow Miss Boo had put behind my head. When I heard Chief McCray clear his throat, I opened my eyes and lifted my head.

"You feel like talking now?" he asked. "Can you tell me what went on here?"

"Yes, of course," I said, keeping my voice soft. I had, after all, experienced a shock. Finding a dead body and seeing all that blood was enough to give anyone the vapors.

At that moment, Miss Boo arrived from the nether regions of the house, a glass of water in her hand. "Here you go, Sissy. You drink a few sips of this nice cool water. It'll perk you right up." She looked up at the uniformed policeman. "I didn't mess with anything. I just opened a cupboard, got a glass, and turned on the water to fill it.

"I was just going to question Miss . . . er . . ." he sputtered to a stop.

"Townley," I said. "Cecelia Townley, but everyone calls me Sissy."

"Were you here with Miss Townley?" he asked Miss Boo. "I'll need to question you separately."

"No, I wasn't here. I came later."

"Why?" he queried. "Why are you here?"

"Because Sissy needed me," she exclaimed, as if he ought to have figured that out for himself. "Sissy is my friend and my tenant. She rents my garage apartment, you know. She is a young person away from home for the first time, and something upsetting has happened to her. It is my duty to watch over her in the absence of her parents." She sounded indignant that he should as much as hint that she shouldn't be there doing her duty, protecting and mothering a young woman away from her own mother.

"Upsetting?" he looked from Miss Boo to me.

"She found a dead body, Chief McCray! A dead body! Surely you can understand that would be distressing to anyone, much less a young person, sheltered from life until she came upon this . . . this . . ."

I used the occasion to wipe a tear from my eye. There was no need for the police chief to know that it was a tear of amusement at Miss Boo's explanation of my sheltered life rather than one of emotion over finding a dead body.

"Miss Townley, what were you doing here?" McCray asked as he cut off Miss Boo's speech in mid-sentence. He pulled a small notebook and a pen from his pocket. He obviously had come to the conclusion he wouldn't get anywhere with Miss Boo.

"I had an appointment to interview Miss Saint Pierre for the *News. The Mount Chapel News,*" I said.

"You're a reporter for the *News*?"

"Yes." That wasn't a lie, not really. I was sort of a reporter. Sort of a receptionist. Sort of an all-around girl Friday.

"So she knew you were coming? You didn't just show up?"

"Well, she might not have known it was me, Sissy Townley, coming, but she knew someone was."

"How? How did she know that?"

"She might have been expecting Marilee Hubbard. I don't know exactly who called who to make the appointment, whether she called Marilee or Merilee called her, or if an agent or representative did it."

"Why would she have called Miss Hubbard?" He frowned.

"Marilee is the society reporter, and she was going to do the interview, but she fell and broke her leg. She's in the hospital in Savannah. My boss, Gene Hoskins, sent me instead."

"I see," he said and frowned some more as he made more notes. "What time did you get here?"

"The appointment was for ten o'clock, and it was close to that when I got here. Maybe a few minutes earlier."

"And someone let you in the front gate?"

"No, it was standing open."

"Is that your car in front? The convertible?" He nodded toward the front of the house. "Or is it yours, Miss Boo?"

"It's mine," I replied.

Just then, more policemen came in the front door and through the entry hall, accompanying a man in medical scrubs. He was carrying a black bag, like doctors on TV. He looked as if he'd been in the middle of surgery when they fetched him to come to the murder scene. They all came into the room where we were and stopped.

"In there, Doc." McCray gestured toward the office door, and they all hurried toward the sight of the murder.

That's what it had to be, didn't it? A murder? I didn't see a gun anywhere. And besides, somebody who appeared to have the ego of LaRue Saint Pierre wouldn't off herself. No way!

McCray turned his attention back to me. "Why were you going to interview Miss . . . ah . . . La Pierre? Who is she?"

"Saint Pierre," Miss Boo corrected him. "LaRue Saint Pierre."

"What kind of name is that?" he muttered. "Sounds made-up to me."

"It was," Miss Boo said. "Her real name was Lorraine Coggins."

He lowered the pen once more and looked at Miss Boo. "She used an alias?" he said, his voice going up in amazement.

"She is . . . was . . . a writer," Miss Boo said. "An author. Many authors use a name other than their own. It's called a 'pen name.'"

He shook his head and made another note. "Go on, Miss Townley," he urged. "You got here about ten o'clock?"

"Yes."

"And the front gate was open? You didn't call up to the house on the phone?"

"No, I didn't call. The gate was standing open, so I just drove up to where I parked."

"But usually you have to call—right? You open the little door in the brick pillar and use the phone to tell somebody that you're here, and if they want to, they open the gate for you?"

"I guess," I answered. "I've never done it, so I don't really know how it works."

"Who let you in the house?"

"Nobody. I rang the doorbell a couple of times before I noticed that the door was open just a little."

"Open?"

"Yes, sir. Just a little," I repeated, and I measured with my fingers, indicating three or four inches.

"And you just walked in?"

"Not exactly. I pushed the door open," I demonstrated with one hand. "Then I called out Miss Saint Pierre's name."

"Did she answer?"

"No."

"She was probably already dead," he commented under his breath as he made more notes. "What did you do then?"

"I walked in. I stood in the middle of the foyer," I waved my hand toward the entrance hall, "and I called her name again."

"No answer?" he asked, looking at me.

"No answer," I agreed. "So I went into the dining room."

"That the room on the other side of the front hall?" He looked in that direction.

"Yes, sir. I thought she might be in in the kitchen having breakfast and hadn't heard me."

"Uh-huh." He didn't look like he believed me.

"I called a couple of times. Still no answer, so I retraced my steps into the front hall, then came in here—in this room—and called again. That's when I thought I heard something."

"You did?" He looked up with interest. "What did you hear? A shot?"

"No. It definitely wasn't a shot. Nothing loud like that. I don't know what it was, but it sounded like it might have come from the direction of the office, so I opened that door . . ." I pointed at the office door, "and I went in."

"That's when you found the body," he said. He didn't ask, he stated it as fact, so I had to correct him.

"Not right off I didn't. I walked in and looked around then called her name again. I was looking at the pictures on the walls. They're the covers of the books she's written, only bigger and in nice frames. I was looking at those, thinking that I ought to mention them in the article I was going to write, and when I moved around the side of the desk, I saw the body."

"Did you touch anything?"

"No, sir. I did not."

"What did you do next?"

"I went outside. I was feeling real . . . wobbly. Faint, I guess. I leaned against my car for a minute before I called 911. Then I sat down on the front step to wait for you."

He turned to Miss Boo. "And how did you find out about it so quickly, Miss Boo? Were you here with Miss Townley when she found the body?"

"I called her," I said. I didn't want Miss Boo pulled into this, but she was here, so there had to be a reasonable explanation. "I was . . ." I tried to think of a reason why I would do such a thing. "I was scared. I was here by myself, and there was a dead body in the house. She came right over to . . ."

"I came to comfort her," Miss Boo said. "To reassure her. She was sitting on the front step when I got here. Walter, Officer Mays, had just gotten here, and he helped me get Sissy into the house before she passed out." She patted me on the hand again.

"I'm going to want to talk to you more later," Chief McCray said as he got up. "You stay here. Don't leave." With that, he went toward the throng of policemen in the next room. I don't know why anyone would think I'd leave after I'd stayed this long. I certainly was going to stay to see and hear everything possible. I had the best possible view of the crime without seeing it actually happen. I had a dilly of a story to write and, hopefully, have my byline on. Not my first, but much more impressive than interviewing the librarian or a store owner.

"Johnson," I heard him say. "Go take fingerprints off the phone at the gate and the gate itself." He started toward the scene of the crime, then he turned toward the policeman who'd taken a couple of steps toward the front door. "The front door, as well. And take this young woman's prints. We'll need to rule them out." He looked at me with a frown. "Or not."

By this time, the house was full of police, some uniformed and others in street clothes. Some went in the office to see the murder scene. Others were just looking around the house. One policeman announced in a loud voice, "We need the civilian cars moved so the coroner can park close to the front door."

"I'll take care of that," a familiar voice said, and Asher Donovan walked in. "Sissy, Granny Boo, since you're both here, am I to assume you're involved in some way?"

"Sissy found the body," Miss Boo said.

"Of course you did," he said, looking at me. "That's what you do, find bodies," he muttered in a snarky tone.

"I had an appointment to interview Miss Saint Pierre," I said for what seemed to be the umpteenth time, "For the paper. Gene Hoskins sent me." I felt it was necessary to explain why I—unimportant Sissy Townley—would be at the home of such a well-known celebrity.

"And you, Granny Boo? You came with her?"

"No, Asher," Miss Boo said, and she sounded peeved. "I didn't come with her. She called because she got scared when she found the body. She had called the police, but she had to wait, all alone, until they got here, so she called me. I came to be with her in . . ." I thought she almost said, "in her hour of need," but that was carrying it a little too far. "Until they got here," she finished.

"You'll need to stay close," Asher said to me. "There'll be more questions. Give me your car keys, and I'll move both vehicles out of the way."

Which is why he wasn't there when the mousy man came in.

CHAPTER SEVEN

I noticed him standing in the foyer, holding a cardboard tray, the kind you use to carry drinks so they won't spill. It had three Styrofoam cups in it, and he bent his slender form forward slightly and held his free hand over them as if to keep them from tumbling over. When I say 'mousy', I mean he resembled a mouse. He was short and his eyes darted this way and that. His hair was gray and thinning, and although I couldn't see his eyes from across the room, I thought they were probably gray as well. His clothing consisted of baggy pants and a wrinkled shirt and was gray, too. Yes, a gray mouse, that's what he was. He even looked as nervous and skittery as a mouse in a room full of people—or cats.

"What's happened?" he squeaked. Well, maybe he didn't squeak. Maybe I only expected him to. But his voice was high and nervous. "Where's my sister?"

"Your sister?" Miss Boo asked.

"Lo . . . er . . . LaRue Saint Pierre," he answered. "She's expecting a reporter from the *Mount Chapel News*, Marilee Hubbard, this morning, to do an interview. Where is she? What's happened?" he repeated.

Suddenly, Miss Boo sprang up from beside me and approached the newcomer. "Milton?" She placed her hand on his arm. "It is Milton, isn't it? I remember you from school. I was friends with your sister, Lily. Remember me? Emily? People called me Boo, you know. They still do."

He looked puzzled, as if trying to figure out what his sister Lily's friend, Emily, was doing here. He looked at her, then at the policemen coming and going, then back at Miss Boo.

"Something's happened, hasn't it? Something bad. Or else there wouldn't be all these police in the house."

He trembled, and Miss Boo grasped his arm with one hand and patted it with the other. Miss Boo was very big on patting people to soothe them. "Let's get away from this crowd, Milton, so we can talk. Let's go into the dining room. It's quiet in there." She tucked her arm under his and drew him with her as she turned away from the police coming and going in the living room. When she looked at me and signaled with her head, I got up and followed them.

"She did something, didn't she? My sister did something to Marilee. I told her . . . I told her to leave Marilee Hubbard alone . . . that the past was the past. 'Just forget it.' That's what I said. 'Remember your reputation. You're a bestselling author. You don't have to prove anything to anyone anymore.' But no, she wouldn't let it drop."

Miss Boo steered him to the far end of the dining room and pulled out a chair. "Sit here, Milton. I have something to tell you, and it's best you sit down."

"Just tell me one thing, Emily. What did she do to Marilee?" he asked as he set the tray of coffee on the dining table and sat down. "Did they get in a fight? Did my sister injure her? She didn't kill her, did she?"

"No, Milton. She didn't kill her. She didn't do anything to Marilee," she said as she pulled out the chair next to him.

"No?"

I swear his nose wiggled as he thought about that.

"She didn't hurt Marilee?"

"No, Milton. She didn't hurt Marilee," Miss Boo confirmed. "Marilee couldn't come do the interview. She had an accident and broke her leg."

"Broke her leg? Did Lorraine do that? Cause the accident?" His nose twitched as he asked the question.

"No, Milton. Not at all." Miss Boo patted his arm again as she reassured him. "Marilee was visiting her sister in Savannah when it happened. She's not even here in Mount Chapel."

"I was going to do the interview," I said, trying to get his mind off the thought of his sister doing harm to another woman. "I'm a reporter with the *News*." My mind was busy with the question he'd asked. Why in the world would LaRue Saint Pierre want to kill the society editor?

"Who are you?" he asked bluntly.

"I'm Sissy Townley," I answered. "Mr. Hoskins sent me in Marilee's place."

"And Lorraine . . . that is, LaRue . . . was okay with that?"

"I don't know," I said. "He just told me to be here at ten o'clock." I was beginning to understand why Gene Hoskins was so nervous when he talked to me. I'll bet he hadn't talked to Miss Saint Pierre—or Miss Coggins, whatever you wanted to call her—about Marilee's accident, and he was sending me into the lion's den unprepared.

Miss Boo was usually unflappable, but I could tell that she was frustrated at not being able to keep the conversation under her control. "Milton," she said firmly. "I need to tell you. . ."

"Tell me what?" he interrupted.

"Lorraine is dead," she blurted out, getting it out there rapidly before she was interrupted again.

Milton didn't say a word. He just stared at Miss Boo, as if he hadn't heard her, or else didn't understand what she was telling him. Finally, he shook his head. "Dead?" he repeated. "Dead?"

"Yes. Sissy found her body when she came to do the interview."

He turned his gaze to me. Wordless, his mouth hung open. His eyes, which I now saw were light blue, not gray, were fixed on me. After a minute, he looked back to Miss Boo. He said one word. "How?"

"She was shot," Miss Boo said.

"Shot," he said, and his eyes glazed over like his thoughts had all turned inward.

They sat there, quietly. Finally, Milton stirred. His eyes started darting this way and that, and he pulled away from Miss Boo's grip on his arm.

"Who did it?" he asked. "Who would want to kill Lorraine?" He reached for one of the cups of coffee, opened the tab, and took a sip before he spoke again. "Lots of people." He answered his own question. "Lots of people would want to kill Lorraine."

"Who indeed?" Police Chief McCray said as he entered. "Who are all these people who would kill Miss Saint Pierre? And who are you? How did you get in here?"

"Chief McCray," Miss Boo said. "This is Lorraine Coggins's brother, Milton Coggins. He planned to be present at the interview for the *News*."

"I have men at the gate to stop people from coming in. How come they didn't bring you to me?"

"I came in the back way," Milton said.

"Back way? There's a back way?" McCray asked.

Milton waved vaguely toward the back of the house. "There's another gate off a side street. It's closest to my house, so I use it instead of coming in the front."

"Excuse me a minute," the chief said. He walked to a policeman standing at the foyer, and I heard him say something about securing a back way into the property before he returned to us.

"Mr. . . .er . . .Coggins?" the police chief said, a question in his voice.

"Yes. Yes. Coggins. Milton Coggins."

"And you are LaRue Saint Pierre's brother?"

"Yes, I am. Her real name is Lorraine Coggins. LaRue Saint Pierre is her pen name."

"Well, I have some bad news about your sister."

"Yes," Milton put his hand over his eyes. "Emily told me."

"Emily?" Chief McCray questioned.

"He means me, Chief," Miss Boo said. "Emily is my real name. Boo is just my nickname."

"Does everybody around here have a fake name?" he muttered. "Saint Pierre. Boo. Sissy." He shook his head. "And you two know each other?" the chief asked, looking back and forth between Miss Boo and Milton Coggins.

"Yes. I was friends with his sister, Lily, when we were in high school. I knew Milton from back then, although he's younger than I am."

"And you knew the victim as well? Lorraine Coggins?" he asked Miss Boo.

"Yes, I did, although not as well as I knew her sister, Lily. And I've told Milton about his sister's death," she said. She reached over and patted Milton's arm once again.

"I'll need to interview you, Mr. Coggins. Where were you this morning before you arrived here?"

"I was home, then I went through a drive-thru to get some coffee, then came in the back way. I knew about the interview, although I was expecting Marilee Hubbard, not this young lady." He waved his hand toward me, the one holding a cup of coffee, and it sloshed out onto the highly polished table where he was sitting. "Oh shi . . ." he started. "Sorry," he said, wiping the drops of liquid off the table with the arm of his shirt. "Lor . . . uh . . . LaRue will throw a fit if . . ." He stopped speaking when it registered that what he was about to say was inappropriate in the circumstances. His sister would no longer throw a fit about spilled coffee or anything else.

CHAPTER EIGHT

Chief McCray told Miss Boo and me we could leave. "Come by the police station later today and sign your statements," he said. "We'll have them typed up in a couple of hours." I thought Miss Boo might come up with some reason why we needed to stay, and I was surprised when she kept quiet. Asher Donovan had returned from moving our cars and was standing just outside the dining room entrance, bouncing my keys in his hand, listening. He offered them as I approached. "You okay with this?" he asked, his sexy hazel eyes roaming my face.

"I'm fine," I said, although I would not be if he looked at me like that much longer. There was a possibility that I would melt. "I'm going to the office," I said and reached for his outstretched hand. Ash played the game that schoolboys often do. As I touched the keys, his fingers closed around mine, trapping me. I would have to struggle to get loose.

"Sure?" he asked. "You've had a shock, finding a body like that." He tugged my hand, pulling me slightly closer to him. "You might need some . . ." he gave a yank and suddenly my body was touching his, "professional attention." His breath warmed my cheek. "Mouth-to-mouth resuscitation," he whispered.

"I'm sure," I answered. I was lying. Being in close proximity to the sexiest man I'd ever been in the same room with never led to being what could be considered 'fine'. In fact, it had, in the past, led to being kissed to within an inch of combustion. But not here. Not at a murder scene.

He released the keys, and I grabbed them and headed toward the front door before he could delay me in any other way. Not that I wouldn't have been happy to be delayed in any other circumstance than this.

When I showed up at the office, Gene Hoskins was watching for me. "What in the h . . . er . . .world is going on at Briarwood? The police scanner is on fire. They're saying there's a four-nineteen and it's a fifty-five A. I'm reading that as being a dead body and it's a homicide. That can't be right, can it? We don't have murders in Mount Chapel."

The small amount of hair still left on the fringes of his skull stood out around his head like a halo. I had never seen my boss so frazzled. "I wanted to call you, but I didn't want to interfere with your interview with Miss Saint Pierre. You did get that, didn't you?"

"No, I didn't," I said, and taking the initiative, I grabbed his arm and started pulling him into his office. "I didn't," I repeated, "but I got something better," I whispered. I turned and closed the door behind us.

"Miss Saint Pierre, or should I say Miss Coggins, is who was murdered, and I found the body."

"What?" He rubbed the top of his bald head, like he had done the day before when he gave me the assignment. "Sissy? Are you okay?" Concern showed on his face.

I didn't know why people kept asking me if I was okay. If I wasn't, I'd fake it until I was. I wasn't okay when my fiancé ran off with another woman, but I faked it and look at me now. I had a job as a newspaper reporter—well, sort of—and I have not one, but two sexy boyfriends. Well, that might be stretching it a bit. Two almost boyfriends.

"I'm fine," I replied. "But maybe I'd better get the story written up. I'm assuming you want it for tomorrow's edition?"

The *Mount Chapel News* was a weekly paper which came out each Friday morning. The issue due out tomorrow was already written—or almost. The only articles not yet submitted were due within a few hours. They would be proofed, set, and tonight, while the rest of the world slept, the paper would be printed. The interview I was to have done was scheduled for next week's edition, but a murder was a different thing altogether. Especially the murder of a famous author, like LaRue Saint Pierre.

"Murdered? You found her?" Hoskins sputtered as he took his seat behind the big, cluttered desk. He reached toward the phone as he said, "I've always wanted to say this. I've imagined it but thought it would never happen." He put the receiver to his ear and punched two buttons on the handset. "Tony! Stop the presses!"

He listened for a few seconds before he said, "I know. I know. It doesn't go to press for a few more hours. I just wanted to say that. But hold whatever you're doing. There's been some breaking news that's going to take a lot of room. Maybe the whole front page. I'll get back to you."

When he hung up, he picked up a pencil and started drumming on the desktop. "Tell me what happened, from the beginning." He listened attentively as I went through the story one more time.

"You'll write it, of course," he said. "We have an empty office where you won't be disturbed. I'll set you up there."

Of course, I'd write it. Who else would write it? Who else *could* write it? I was the one who saw everything. "I was wondering, should I include the fact that LaRue Saint Pierre is a pen name? That her real name is Lorraine Coggins and that she's a native of Mount Chapel?"

"Really? She's a Mount Chapel native? Yes, it's time for that secret to be out. You mention it, but I'll get someone else to write a piece about the family—about her parents and siblings. I don't remember. . . ." He drifted off, deep in thought for a few seconds, then said, "I sent Porter Quinn to see what was going on. Maybe he'll get some pictures."

"Oh, I almost forgot. I have lots of pictures," I said and pulled out my phone. "I took several of the room and of the body."

"The body?" he exclaimed. "You actually have pictures of the body?"

"Yes. She . . . er . . . her body was in the office, behind the desk. I took pictures of everything in the room." I punched the right buttons to bring up the photos and handed my phone to him. "There ought to be something on there we can use. Tell me which ones you want, and I'll send them to the *News* by way of telephone."

No way was I going to let my boss have control of my whole phone, not with me going into another room to write. He picked several—one of the body, one from the side of the desk that showed only her hand, and a couple of the whole room from different angles.

"These will do," he said. "I don't think we should run the one that shows the bloody body, but I took it anyway. I'll think about it. We'll have the rights to all of them."

"We?" I asked.

"We," he said firmly. "You were on assignment, so technically, those photos are property of the *Mount Chapel News*." He looked at me, as if to say, "Do you understand, Sissy?"

"Yes, sir," I answered the silent question.

I gathered my laptop from my desk at the front of the newsroom, got a soda from the vending machine in the break room, and met my boss at a small office toward the rear of the building.

"You'll be able to work in here," he said, picking up a square of cardboard from the desktop. "I'll put this sign on the door and nobody will bother you." Someone had written "Working! Do not interrupt!" in black marker on what appeared to be part of a shipping box. He attached it to a clip on the outside of the door and pulled it closed behind him.

Wow! My first big assignment. I looped my fingers together and stretched my hands and arms out, my mind going lickety-split in a dozen different directions. How to start?

It didn't seem long before Mr. Hoskins stuck his head in the door. "How are you coming, Sissy?"

"I'm almost finished," I answered and typed a few more words. "There. See what you think."

He came to lean over my shoulder and read what was on the screen. "Send it to my office," he said as he turned away. "Boo came by to see you, but I told her you were working and couldn't be disturbed." He paused at the door. "She gave me the impression that she was there at the scene as well." He didn't say another word, just looked at me like he expected an answer.

"Yes, sir. I called her while I was waiting on the police to get there. She came to . . ." I had to think a minute. Why had she come? Because something exciting had happened. Because Miss Boo had to be in the middle of things. Because . . . "to settle my nerves. I was upset over finding . . . you know . . . a dead body."

Gene Hoskins nodded his head. That answer had satisfied him, although I'm sure he knew as well as I did that Boo Bryce came because she wasn't going to be left out of any goings-on in Mount Chapel, especially something as exciting as the murder of a famous author who had returned to her hometown to show off her new wealth and fame.

CHAPTER NINE

My daddy had all kinds of sayings that he used that don't make a bit of sense to most people. He read a lot, and if he came across something he didn't understand, he looked it up on the internet and found out what it meant, and he'd start saying it himself. There's a lot that Daddy said that I didn't understand, but usually I just let it slide. I had enough stuff floating around in my head without thinking about his oddball expressions.

He used the expression "you can't keep 'em down on the farm" as long as I could remember, and one day I finally I asked him, "Daddy, what does that have to do with anything? We don't live on a farm, and nobody's trying to keep anybody anywhere."

So he explained that it was part of a line from a song that had been popular a hundred years ago, during the First World War. "The whole line," he said, is 'you can't keep 'em down on the farm after they've seen Paree.'" Which didn't make any more sense to me than it did to start with.

"So?" I said, looking at him right hard.

"It's about the boys who went off to war in France, and when they got back home, those who lived through it, they had seen and done so much that their lives would never be the same. They'd been to Paris, France, and maybe London, England, and New York City. They'd seen things the people back home never would. They'd never be happy down on the farm after seeing the world."

When I thought about it awhile, it made sense, sort of. And it popped into my head Monday morning when I went back to work at my regular job, the front desk of the *Mount Chapel News*. In the last few days, I had been trusted to do an interview with a famous person, and I had found a dead body . . . the body of said famous person.

It didn't matter that I never got to the interview part. What mattered was that my boss entrusted me with the job. And even if I hadn't done the interview, I had written a front-page story about the murder and had a byline that followed the story onto big city newspapers. People all over the country could read what I had written, followed by my name: Cecelia Townley.

I had just connected the fifth caller of the day to classified advertising and one disgruntled person to circulation. "I pay good money to get a copy of the *Mount Chapel News* every week and dad-blame it, I ought to get one," he had yelled loud enough that somebody in circulation should have heard him over my phone.

That's when Daddy's saying popped into my head. I had been doing exciting things. Finding a murder victim. Being interviewed by the police. Seeing first hand as the police started their investigation of the murder. Writing an important story. Would I ever again be satisfied with just answering the phone and writing about the new books at the library?

I had seen Paree, figuratively. Now I was back on the farm—that is, the reception desk at the front door of the weekly paper, and my job was no longer writing about an unsolved murder, but answering the telephone and fielding questions from callers and people who came in the front door, all of which was very humdrum.

Of course, it all depended on who walked in the front door. When it's police detective Asher Donovan, it was the perfect place to be. He folded his arms and propped himself up on the counter that was meant to hold the current issue of the paper, message pads, pens that advertised the *Mount Chapel News*, and to stop irate customers from getting too close to me, the innocent receptionist who was only there to direct traffic, so to speak.

"Hi," he said and smiled. Just that alone was enough to blow me away. Or maybe melt me. Whatever.

"Hi," I replied. Foxy, huh? "Can I help you?" I asked as I stood up and took the two steps between my desk and the front counter.

"I don't know. Can you?" he said, and one of his fingers, the right pointer, I thought, reached over and ran over the top of my hand where it was laying on the counter. I thought I blushed. Me. Sissy Townley, the girl who could put down the most shameless flirt in my whole high school with a few well-chosen words, was blushing. And the most embarrassing thing was that he knew it. Knew that I was blushing. Knew that he had shook me up.

This would never do. I frowned at him. Unfortunately, he had rattled me from the get-go, so I had no control over what came out of my mouth. "It depends on what you want," I said. Big mistake. He just looked at me and smiled his lopsided smile, the one with a little lift at one side of his mouth, and said nothing.

It took a few seconds for my mind to catch up with my mouth. When it did, my blush increased, which irritated me to no end, because it immediately marked me as an innocent school-girl, which I wasn't. I was a twenty-three-year-old woman who, as my father would have said, knew the score. Except Daddy would never have said it about his daughter. In his loving eyes, I would be innocent until I married.

"Who are you here to see?" I asked in a firm voice that was meant to convey to Asher Donovan that he should straighten up and behave himself. This was a place of business, after all, and not an appropriate place to play handsies.

"You." His answer upset my carefully held self-confidence.

"Me?" I squeaked.

"You." His eyes—dare I use the term—twinkled as he studied my face. Then his demeanor changed and his finger stopped its exploration of the back of my hand. He pulled back about an inch as he spoke. "I need to ask you some more questions concerning . . . Oh, hello, Mr. Hoskins," he said in a different tone of voice than the one he'd been using. He took a couple of steps toward my boss, who'd approached from the depths of the newsroom, probably when he noticed the police detective talking with me. My attention had been glued to the handsome policeman in front of me and the finger tracing a pattern on the back of my hand, and I hadn't even seen my boss approaching.

Gene Hoskins had a tentative smile on his face as he advanced. "Detective Donovan, what brings you our way this morning?" he asked as they shook hands.

"Well, sir, I was going over Miss Townley's statement again when some more questions occurred to me. I need to follow up on something she said."

"Certainly, certainly, Asher. Anything we can do to help."

"I came by to find out when she would be free. I need to take her back to the scene of the crime. Have her retrace her steps."

"Sissy is free to go with you anytime you need. She can go right now, if that's what you want." His eyebrows went up and down as he looked from Ash to me and back again. "The *News* is always ready to help our police in any manner we can. Sissy, you run along and help Detective Donovan. Don't worry about the time. Do what you need."

"Yes, sir," I said. "I'll just get my purse." I walked the few steps back to my desk.

"I'll wait for you at my car," Ash said. "Thanks, Mr. Hoskins. This will help in the investigation." He offered his hand to my boss again. "I'll bring her back when I'm through with her."

When I heard that statement, my mind bounced around in directions it wouldn't do to verbalize, and I'm sure my face got even redder. My purse was in the bottom drawer of my desk, on the side away from the counter, which made it a bit easier to hide for a few seconds, as I tried to pull my thoughts away from what "when I'm through with her" might be construed to mean.

Asher strode to the exit and pushed the glass door open, then turned toward me and shot me one of his sexy smiles, the kind that could turn me into a puddle of mush, if mush could make a puddle, and if I let it. Through the front window, I saw the unmarked car he drove sitting in the no parking zone directly in front of the entrance. Of course, he wouldn't get a ticket like an ordinary person. All the police force knew what he drove. He was one of them, after all.

Gene Hoskins watched him go out the door, then sidled over to me. "Find out all you can, Sissy. Find out if they have any suspects, who they're looking at and what the motive for the murder might be. Maybe you can write a follow up piece for this week's paper." He started toward the back of the room when he stopped and turned around.

"Maybe we can submit it to the big boys in Jackson or Memphis, since we won't be publishing for a few days." He started walking again, then stopped once more. "Don't worry about not being here. As long as you're with Asher Donovan, consider the time you spend as job related."

Gene Hoskins didn't know what he was giving me permission for. I'd gladly spend time with the hunky detective, job related or not.

CHAPTER TEN

When I exited, Asher Donovan was waiting for me. Leaning up against the side of his car, he looked like a model in a magazine. Whatever he was selling, I'd buy it. So would every red-blooded woman under the age of . . . shoot . . . at any age! Even in everyday clothing instead of the biker attire he wore when he was working undercover, he still had that "bad boy" vibe and was as sexy as all get-out. A breeze ruffled his hair, making it look as if somebody had been running their hands through it. Like me. Like I'd been running my hands through his longish tresses. I wondered if he was letting it grow again in preparation for another undercover assignment. When Miss Boo and I had returned from the Gulf Coast after being rescued by her sexy grandson, Ash had his shoulder-length hair cut and styled to what was more appropriate for a police officer, and he'd kept it short these few months that he'd remained in Mount Chapel, doing small-town police stuff.

"Ready to go?" he asked as he stood away from the car. "Your boss tell you to pump me for all the information you can find out about the case?"

"Yeah," I said and grinned. "He did, but I already knew to do that."

He opened the door and stood aside until I slid into the passenger seat then slammed it behind me.

This was only the second time I'd been in a car with Asher Donovan. The first was when he showed up at the Biloxi jail to rescue me and Miss Boo from being arrested for the murder of the man we'd found, dead, in the bushes outside the elegant hotel and casino where we were staying. That time he was dressed in biker garb and drove my little blue convertible like a bat out of hell, as the saying goes, in order to lose the person or persons he said were tailing us.

So here we were, him driving and me riding shotgun, and I'd found another dead body. Maybe that was why I subconsciously expected Ash to drive like he did after the first experience, but I was disappointed, or else relieved. I don't know which. He drove through the Mount Chapel business district, out a main thoroughfare, zig-zagged through some side streets—all while driving within the speed limit—and ended up at the scene of the crime.

He hadn't let the similar circumstances pass. "This is getting to be a habit for you," he said. "Finding dead bodies."

"I hope there won't be any more."

"Some people are just magnets for trouble," he said as he drove slowly up the long drive from the street to the mansion where famous novelist LaRue Saint Pierre, otherwise known as hometown girl Lorraine Coggins, had lived.

The gate at the entrance was standing open, but signs were prominently affixed to the brick columns on both sides. "NO ADMITTANCE," they said, and in smaller letters underneath. "BY ORDER OF MOUNT CHAPEL POLICE DEPARTMENT." Yellow crime scene tape was wrapped around each pillar and fluttered in the gentle wind. You couldn't miss the signs or the tape, but I doubted it would keep curiosity seekers out.

"Do those signs do any good?" I asked.

"Probably not," Ash answered. "But we're in and out of here too often to have to bother with locking the gate, and we don't have enough personnel to station someone out here full time."

"You don't have civilian assistants of some sort? Like junior police or senior citizen auxiliary or someone?"

He looked at me. "That's an idea. Play cops. Maybe give them tin badges to wear. Do you think the bad guys would mind what they say?" His tone of voice was somewhere between teasing and sarcastic.

"No, but looky-loos would. And if they had walkie-talkies, they could call for help if they needed it. It beats people coming in and wandering around the place, messing up footprints and picking up clues to keep as souvenirs."

He frowned, but he didn't answer me. Too macho, I reckoned, to accept a suggestion from a woman, and a civilian at that.

He circled the fountain and pulled up by the steps leading up to the front door. "This is about where you were parked, isn't it?" He looked at me for an answer. "Before I moved your car out of the way?"

"Yes, right about here," I answered.

He reached over and opened the glove box.

I always wondered why they called that cubby a 'glove' box. Nobody keeps gloves in it, but maybe they did a hundred years ago, and they just kept on calling it that. Personally, I keep the car registration papers in mine, and an ice scraper, although that isn't needed down here in the southern part of the state like it was back home. But if we get a sudden ice storm in Southern Mississippi, I'm prepared. And I keep a little zippered bag of emergency supplies, like a bottle of ibuprofen, a Band-Aid or two, a tampon, and way down in the bottom there's a couple of foil wrapped . . . er. . . necessities, in case my former fiancée didn't have any. Why they're still there in my stash, I don't know. Wishful thinking, maybe. They'll probably be dried up by the time I get another boyfriend who I consider serious enough to use them with.

So anyway, Asher opened the glove box, reached in, and pulled out a fistful of . . . would you believe. . . gloves. Latex gloves. He shoved them into his pocket as he got out of the car.

As we opened the car doors, a uniformed cop opened the front door and stepped out. Seeing me first, he started speaking. "I'm sorry, ma'am, but you can't . . ." he said before catching sight of Ash. "Oh, it's you, sir. I thought it was another nosy. . . ."

"We have to do something better than this, Hobbs, to keep the lookers out. See if you can't get that police auxiliary group to come man the front gate. We'll be lucky if we don't have tourists all over the place once the word spreads about who the victim was."

"Yes, sir," Hobbs said and pulled a phone from his belt.

"Have them man the back entrance too. If the public doesn't know about it now, they'll find out, and it won't be long before they'll be sneaking in that way as well."

Hobbs nodded as he spoke into his cell phone. I guess my suggestion wasn't so bad after all.

"So, you went up these steps . . ." He was taking it step by step, literally.

"Yes, and I stopped here by the doorbell," I said and pointed at the round button located in a brass panel, below which was a grid of metal, obviously a speaker so someone inside the house could question the person at the door. "And I rang it."

"Rang?" Ash questioned.

"Rang," I answered. "I heard it. Chimes."

"And?"

"And nothing. Nobody came. Nobody answered."

"What did you do next?"

"Rang it again."

"Still nobody." This time it wasn't a question. It was a statement.

"Right. But that time it occurred to me that I heard the chime quite loudly. It was too loud for the door to be closed. I looked at the door and sure enough, it was standing open."

"How open?" Ash asked.

"Not much. About three or four inches," I said, measuring with my fingers. He reached around me and, taking hold of the knob, pulled the door toward us until it was about the width I had indicated.

"About like this?"

"Yes. That's about right."

He turned and pushed the button. Melodic tones sounded from somewhere in the house. Eight notes announced our presence, and we listened as they faded away. Yes, I counted. There were eight.

"Then what did you do?"

"I used one finger and pushed it open." I stuck out my pointer finger and demonstrated. The door swung open easily, and the foyer appeared to be identical to what it had been the week before. Formal. Regal. The elegant red roses on the table must have been fake, because they looked as fresh as they had days earlier.

"Did you walk in?"

"Yes, just a little."

He put a hand under my elbow and urged me in. I stopped after two or three steps, and Ash looked at me, eyebrows raised.

"I stopped about here and called." I demonstrated, my voice raised to the level it had been that day. "Miss Saint Pierre?"

"Did you hear anything? I'm assuming she was already dead and didn't answer you."

"Right. I didn't hear anything at that point."

"At any point?"

"Yes, later I thought I did."

"But now?"

"I may have called out again. I thought . . ." I trailed off.

"Thought what?"

"That she might have gone to the bathroom. That's what women do sometimes. Go right before you have somewhere to go or something to do. So that you don't have to stop and go during, if you get my drift."

"I got it. What did you do next?"

"I walked over to the dining room," I said and nodded that direction.

"Why did you go that way?"

"No reason," I said. "It was just one way or the other, and I chose the dining room way."

"Did you actually go into the room?"

"I don't remember. If I did, it was only a step or two. I admired all the fancy stuff in there—the painting and all," I said and took a couple of steps to demonstrate.

"Uh-huh." He didn't sound like he believed me.

"Well, I didn't exactly *admire* it. I just looked at it."

Ash looked up at the nude woman decorating the wall and grinned that lopsided grin of his. "And then?"

"I turned around and went back to the foyer." I shook my head as I looked around the dining room. Everything appeared to be the same as it had been that morning. "I can't see that anything I'm telling you is helping."

"Not yet it isn't, but let's keep going," he said. His hand gripped my elbow, and he gently changed my direction so we returned to the foyer before he released it. "What did you do next?" he asked as he looked down at me.

"Walked over to the entrance to the living room," I answered, and did it, Asher following along. "I stood here looking around, and finally I went in."

"Was there a reason that you hesitated? Why you didn't want to go into the living room immediately?"

I looked around the room and tried to project myself back to that day. Why had I hesitated? "Because . . ." I tried to think about my reasoning. "Because the carpet was so perfect," I remembered, "and so deep . . . I knew I'd leave footprints where I walked. And I wondered why people had carpet like that. It would never be perfect. As soon as somebody walked over it, it wouldn't be that way any longer." I looked down at the pale pink fibers, squashed flat by the dozens of people who had walked on it since that day, and recalled my thoughts at the time. "But finally, I did."

Asher frowned. "It was pristine when you first arrived? No footprints?"

That's when it hit me. No footprints leading to the office door. Not LaRue Saint Pierre's footprints. Not the murderer's footprints. So how did they get into the office?

"No," I answered. "No footprints."

CHAPTER ELEVEN

"We'll think about that later," Ash said, holding up one finger. "For now, let's keep retracing your steps. You walked into this room and . . .?"

"And I walked over to about here," I said, approaching the center of a square with a plushy rose-pink sofa forming one side, two velvet chairs making another, and a white love seat on the third. "And I called out again. I sort of yelled her name, and my name, and that I was from the newspaper, and I was here to interview her." I looked back at Asher, who had released his hold on my elbow as he followed me into the room.

"And?" he asked.

"And that's when I heard something. Or thought I did."

"Ahh . . ." Ash said. "You didn't mention that before."

"I haven't? Well, I'm mentioning it now. There was this . . . sound. Not loud enough to call it a noise, but something."

"From where?"

"The office," I said, gesturing in that direction. "So I went to the door, which was closed," I said as I walked to the next place in my story. Ash followed me and grasped the door knob, which showed signs of fingerprint dust all over it, and pulled it shut.

"So you . . .?"

"Knocked on it and called out again."

"Think about this, Sissy. Tell me what kind of sound it was. Could it have been a gun shot?"

"No, not anything that loud." I closed my eyes and thought about it. "Maybe some kind of scraping sound."

"Okay."

"And a click."

"A click?"

"Yes. Like a door latch, or something like that." I just stood there, eyes closed, thinking about the sound. Asher waited for me to continue.

Finally, he prodded me as he had before. "So you . . .?"

"Opened the door," I opened my eyes and completed his sentence.

Once again, he waited for me to say more, but I was reliving it in my mind, trying to recall everything in the order it happened, until he nudged me. "Is that when you saw the body?"

"No, not at first. She was behind the desk." I took a few steps into the room. "I went in and walked around a little and looked at the framed book covers." I demonstrated, taking the same steps I had that day, as near as I could recall. "And when I got to this point, that's when I saw her—Miss Saint Pierre. And I went outside and called the police." I didn't leave out much. It wasn't really important that I'd taken the time to take pictures of everything: the body and the room. And it wasn't important that I'd looked around after I'd discovered the body instead of before. It was all there in my recitation, just maybe not quite in the order it happened.

The room looked as it had the last time I saw it . . . almost. The office chair, a high-backed white leather model, had been moved. Now, several days later, I imagined that Miss Saint Pierre had stood up, been shot, and, when she fell, the chair pushed backward a bit. Probably, the police had moved the chair away from the previous spot in order to get closer to the body. Nothing else had changed from what I remembered.

Asher was silent as he walked around the room, looking at the crime scene. His brow was furrowed. Something was bothering him. "You . . ." he started, then paused, and, like I did, he closed his eyes, imagining as if he were seeing the way it was that day. "The noise you heard, you're sure it came from this room?" He opened his eyes and looked at me, and I nodded. "Then it must have been caused by someone or something in this room, something the killer did."

What he was going to say had occurred to me as well.

"Then where did the killer go? How did he get out of this room without me seeing him?" I thought out loud.

"Exactly," he agreed. He looked around. "And I don't see any place for somebody to hide and sneak out later."

I didn't either. There was no place large enough for anyone to hide. No more doors to provide another exit or a closet. No large cabinets. Just bookcases, not nearly large enough to hold a person. Just then, another incongruity occurred to me. "And how did they get into the office without leaving footprints on that freshly vacuumed carpet? That's what almost stopped me from entering the parlor when I got here." I waved my hand toward the room we'd just come through. "The carpet was so perfect, not a footprint on it, but I didn't want to mess it up by walking on it, but I finally did." The memory of that day was slowly coming back in more detail. "I thought Miss Saint Pierre must have another door, a back way, into the office or library or whatever it is, and when I opened the door and entered, I just assumed I was wrong about hearing anything, and then I found her body, and . . ."

"That must be the answer," Asher said.

"What?"

"There must be another way in and out of this room."

CHAPTER TWELVE

Asher reached in his pocket and pulled out a handful of the gloves he'd retrieved from his glove box. Handing me a couple, he advised, "Better put these on before we look." I wanted to ask, "look where?" and I didn't. Giving me the gloves and instructing me to put them on was his unspoken consent to my inclusion into the investigation, but I wasn't going to do anything to point that out. When he got his gloves on, he walked over to the built-in shelving that covered the back wall.

Painted white, the shelves of the bookcases were edged with fancy trim and a carved top trim that made them look elegant. There were vases and little statues and all sorts of what my mother would call "knick-knacks" and my father would call "folderol" on most of the shelves. The books I saw were the ones by LaRue Saint Pierre. I would have thought there would be lots of books of all kinds. Books to research things she wrote about. Volumes that described the locations where she placed her stories, travel books, and ones about castles and cruise ships and all sorts of exotic places, but I didn't see any. There were a few other volumes, but they didn't look like reference books. They were more like "show off" volumes, covered with dark leather and gold trim.

Asher started at one end of the wall of bookcases. Of course! I'd seen a magazine spread about a door disguised as a section of shelves full of books. But how did you figure out which one was actually a door? And how would you get it open? Asher was running his hand over the sides of the vertical boards that divided the shelves into sections approximately three feet wide. I started at the other end, doing the same thing he was. I didn't know exactly what I was looking for. I guess I was expecting some clue to jump out and bite me.

I had covered two sections of shelves without finding anything that would indicate the presence of a disguised door, and I had started on the third when Ash spoke.

"I bet this one is it."

I stopped what I was doing and walked over to where he stood. I couldn't see any difference between the section he was studying and the ones on either side.

"The trim above the top shelf doesn't quite line up," Ash said as he pointed. "It's a little bit lower on this section."

I saw what he was talking about. Unless you were studying it, you would overlook the minor difference. "But the wider trim at the very top is one piece that doesn't appear to break between sections of bookcase," I said. "You'd never notice the inconsistency if you weren't looking for it."

"You're right about that," he agreed. "You'd have to know it was there, and even then . . ." His words trailed off.

"You might think that the cabinetmaker was off by a half-inch or so," I said. "That small amount isn't suspicious."

"It wouldn't be if every other segment wasn't so accurate." He studied the section of shelves before him. "Now," Asher said, "we need to figure out how to open it."

I ran my hand up and down the wooden trim between the sections of shelves. It all felt firmly attached. Ash did the same thing on the other side. "Nothing there," he said as he finished his side.

"Maybe a switch or hook or something behind the books," I suggested. The shelves held a mixture of curios, obviously expensive items mixed with trivial gewgaws, alternating shelf space with the books that were meant to impress. Those volumes looked more expensive, with leather covers and gold trim. They weren't meant to be read, only to make the shelves look classy and elegant. It occurred to me that depending on the angle, any photo taken of the author sitting at her desk would either have her own books behind her, or, for a more serious portrait, pretentious volumes as would suit a serious writer.

I was working my way from the right side, while Asher took the left. I lifted each little vase, each carved box, every knick-knack, with no success. There was nothing under or behind anything either of us touched.

"It must have something to do with the books," Asher said. "That's all that's left." He took a large red leather-bound volume from the shelf and peered behind it. "Nothing there," he said. I started at the other end of the same row.

We had finished with the shelf that was slightly above our eye level and started on the one below it when I ran into trouble. The third book I tried wouldn't slide out as the previous ones had. I tugged. It resisted. Suddenly, when I moved my fingers to the top of the spine and pulled harder, the book tipped. The spine remained firmly attached to the shelf at the bottom, but the whole thing tilted, and I heard a loud click.

"Oh!" The surprise drew a startled sound from me.

"What?" Ash asked.

I was peering into the spot the red-leather tome now left open. "I think I found something," I said, and he immediately moved behind me, looking over my shoulder. "That," I said as I moved my head out of the way so he could see what I was talking about.

"It looks like a doorbell," Ash said.

"A button behind a book must be there for a purpose," I said. "It wouldn't be there for no reason. Why would you hide a doorbell?"

"Try pushing it," he suggested.

"You think?" My voice reflected a bit of snark as I reached to do what I would have done anyway. When my finger pressed it, there was a click, and the section of shelves swung back about six inches, like a door opening.

We stood there for a few seconds, absorbing what had just happened. Asher gave a long, low whistle, then reached over my shoulder and placed his hand on the bookcase. When he paused and took a deep breath, I put my hand just below his, and together we slowly pushed.

It worked just like a door would, albeit a door covered with shelves of books. The rasping sound reminded me. "That's what I heard!" I said. "That's the sound I heard that morning, that scraping noise."

"Probably someone making an escape," Ash said. "This is how somebody got in and out without leaving tracks in the living room carpet."

CHAPTER THIRTEEN

We stood there, frozen, staring into the darkness beyond. After a few seconds, Asher said, "I'm going to get a flashlight out of my car. I'll be right back." He turned and went toward the door to the living room. At the last second, he paused. "I doubt there's any danger in there, but just to be safe, stay out until I come back."

Usually, I'm a cautious person. Well, semi-cautious, anyway. In some instances. In others, not so much. The longer Asher was gone, the braver I became. First, I stuck my head in, but I couldn't see much. The room I was standing in—the library, I guess you'd call it—had two windows. They were tall and wide, but there were vines growing around them and they didn't bring in enough daylight to help much. If I'd brought my purse inside, I'd have a small flashlight I carry for emergencies. But I'd left it in Ash's car, so I didn't have that handy item.

What could happen? It was a room. A room in a large, expensive home. Not a hovel with holes in the floor or poisonous snakes or anything else that the characters in scary movies deal with. This was real life, and nothing was going to . . . well, I wasn't going to start imagining things. I took a tentative step into the mysterious space. I still couldn't see much, so I took another. My eyes gradually became adjusted to the dark and I could make out forms, but not well enough to tell what they were. *Maybe it's better to stay close to the . . . what would you call it? The door? The bookcase?*

I was pondering the situation when Asher came back from his car. "Do you ever listen?" he said, his voice sounding like he was irritated. He turned the flashlight on and took a cautious step into the room, flashing light before him.

"I listened," I said. "And then I decided to see what was in here. What could happen? This is a perfectly normal house. There's not going to be a bomb or something.

Evidently somebody, at least the murderer, has been coming and going this way."

"A booby trap. That's what could happen. If you step the wrong way or touch the wrong thing you might blow up something. Not like a bomb, exactly, but you could get hurt," he said and took another step, flashing light this way and that.

I hadn't thought about booby traps, ones that the murderer knew how to avoid, so I didn't have a comeback answer.

"And at the very least," he continued as he took another step into the newly discovered room, "you could destroy evidence."

"Well . . ." I mumbled. I hadn't thought about evidence, but I wasn't about to acknowledge he had a point.

As Ash flashed a beam of light around, my eyes adjusted to the darkness. It was a small room, long and narrow. Small enough that without studying the floor plan of the house it would be easy to miss the fact that there was space unaccounted for between the parlor and whatever was to the back of the house. The shaft of light played along the wall, and he zeroed in on a switch to the side of the entrance we had stepped through. Ash used his gloved hand to flip it and light illuminated the area. Overhead, sparkles thrown off by a small but glittering light fixture danced on the ceiling, and against the wall we'd just stepped through, a desk held a lamp, a computer, a printer, a pad of paper, and a jar holding a selection of pens and pencils. As Ash walked around the room, looking closely at the walls, I leaned forward to read the notes scribbled on the top sheet, but I couldn't make out what it said.

"Surely, she didn't come in here to write her books," I said.

"I wouldn't think so," Asher said.

"She has that lovely office—the one we just came through. Why would she come in this cramped place? It looks like it would stifle the imagination."

"Maybe it does just the opposite," he said as he reached the far end of the room, where a closed door indicated more mysteries. "Maybe she writes better with no distractions."

"Maybe," I replied, but I didn't believe this hidden room was conducive for turning out best-selling books with wild plots set in fabulous places.

Ash stood in front of the newly discovered door, his gloved hand on the knob, and looked back around the area. His eyebrows were raised as he studied his surroundings, then he turned the brass handle and, with the slightest effort, the door swung inward.

Long tendrils of vines formed a screen, and I thought it must render the entrance almost invisible from the outside. Asher lightly pushed his hand through the mass of green and easily moved the drapery of leaves aside, enough that a person could slip through, either coming or going. I wanted to know what was on the other side, and when I snuggled close to his side in order to see better, I caught a whiff of his aftershave, a tangy scent suitable for him, better than something sweet. I admit that I liked the feel of his shirt under my cheek as I pressed against him, and I just about forgot that I was supposed to be looking for clues to a murder.

"Let's go outside and see what it looks like from there," he said, taking a step back and breaking contact. It felt sort of...something. Like lonesome, maybe. He smiled down at me, as if he recognized that the closeness had affected me. For just a couple of seconds, I thought he was going kiss me, and I was disappointed when he turned and started toward the opening where we had entered minutes before.

We traced our steps back through the room where the body had been found, the plushy pink living room, and the foyer. Outside, Officer Hobbs was standing at the top of the steps leading up to the front door. He nodded as we descended, and we headed toward the corner of the house. "Need any help, sir?" he asked.

"Not at the moment," Ash answered. "Just don't let anybody in except those who are authorized."

"Yes, sir."

We went around the corner and down the side of the house. Ivy spread over the bricks, framing the windows that looked into the elegant living room, and about fifteen feet farther along were the two windows that furnished daylight to the room where LaRue Saint Pierre's body had been found. A few feet more, the ivy was so dense it became hard to see the wall beneath the tangle of vines and leaves. A couple of feet away from the house, neatly trimmed bushes formed a barrier. They were close together and sufficient to prevent a person from getting close to the windows and gaining a view into the room inside. A few feet farther, however, it changed a bit, appearing to have a spot where a bush had died sometime in the distant past, leaving a gap. It was deceiving, however. Strands of ivy trailed nearly to the ground, skillfully hiding the door behind, and the step beneath the opening was covered with leaves, as if the area did not get raked. Altogether, the disguise worked well. Unless you knew it was there, the entrance (or exit, if you looked at it that way) would go unnoticed. A hidden room. A hidden door. Who knows what else we might find? Excitement was flowing through my veins and I was ready to look for more mysteries.

CHAPTER FOURTEEN

"Sissy, we need to keep this a secret for now. Understand?" Ash gave me a look that said he was serious. "You can't write about it. Not yet, anyway. Until we catch the killer, you can't tell anyone about the room or this entrance."

"Hmm." I was conflicted. I could imagine the headline now. *Secret Room Found in Dead Author's Home!* Followed by my byline. (That's the name of the person who wrote the column or article.) *Does it Hold Clues to Who Killed Her?*

"Understand?" he repeated more firmly.

If I didn't agree, I wouldn't be privy to any other discoveries. "Okay," I said. "If you'll let me know when I *can* write about it. I get the scoop on this."

"Agreed," he said. "Let's go back inside through the front door. I want the forensic guys to look at this before any clues are lost." He backed away, but not before scanning the ground in front of the hidden doorway. "If the murderer came and left this way, there may be footprints, as well as fingerprints on the doorknob and facings."

"Unless they wore gloves, like we are."

"Right," he agreed. "Unless they wore gloves."

We entered the front door, where Hobbs was still standing guard, and proceeded to the library, where the entry by way of the bookcase was still standing open, revealing the room we'd recently discovered. I was ready to explore, see if the secret chamber held any more surprises, but Ash reached out and stopped me. "We have to be extra careful," he said, "or we might destroy a clue. Most likely, this is the way the killer entered and exited. He came in by way of that hidden door to the outside, killed her, and left the same way."

"I'll be careful, I promise," I agreed. *If I'm careful, and if I stay on his good side, maybe I'll find out even more,* I thought.

Before we took a step into the newly discovered room, Ash pulled out his phone and punched a button. "We need somebody from forensics out here at the Saint Pierre site. Yes, again. I've found more." When he put the phone back in his pocket, he looked at me. "Remember, don't touch anything," he said then took a step toward the opening where the section of shelves opened into the secret space.

It looked even spookier than it had earlier. Due to the heavy curtain of ivy that disguised the entrance, the open door to the outside didn't add much illumination, and the sparkling chandelier overhead didn't offer much help.

"The lamp on the desk," I pointed out, "can we turn it on?"

"You still have on your gloves?"

"Yes."

"Okay, then turn it on, but be careful. Don't move anything."

Duh! I knew that. I switched the lamp on as Ash began shining his flashlight around the walls, searching for any more abnormalities, like the one that had pointed us toward this room. I used his distraction to use my phone to snap some pictures of the items on the desk then slipped it back into my pocket before he could tell me not to.

Satisfied with what I'd done so far, I looked around the rest of the room, slowly walking the perimeter, scanning the walls as Asher was doing. Getting a feel of the space.

There was no extra furniture, just the desk and the accompanying chair. No knick-knacks or shelves to hold them. No display of the author's books like there was in the library. The only sign that tied the space to LaRue Saint Pierre was a frayed poster of a book cover thumb-tacked to the wall. If a person were sitting at the desk, perhaps writing on the computer, they could swivel around to look at the image on the opposite wall, but it was hardly inspiring.

The space was a place to work and nothing more. But why would she work in this boring lair instead of the comfortably swank room that we'd come through to reach this secret room? I would've thought Miss Saint Pierre would have preferred more luxury. This room was plain and unadorned except for the oriental rug covering the floor and the scruffy poster on the wall. Even the desk and chair were plain-Jane, low-end furniture—practical instead of decorative. That made sense, in a twisted kind of way. Who would decorate a room that nobody ever saw? Standing by the entrance to the library, I let the essence of the place seep into my thought process.

Seldom used. Almost bare, it would be a bland, dreary place to work. There was nothing to spur the imagination. I walked over to the large copy of the book cover pinned to the wall with plastic-topped thumbtacks and ran my hand over the curling edges, smoothing the tattered paper as best as I could, but try as I might, it wouldn't stay flat. Why? Because something, some bump on the wall underneath protruded just enough to prevent my attempts. Starting at the corner, I rolled the slick paper. It quickly became obvious that the motion had been done many times before, and that was why there were rips and tears along those edges.

When I uncovered a few inches of wall, there was another discovery: a button like the one that opened the hidden door from the library to this hidden room. "Ash," I called. "Come look at this!"

He had just rounded the corner, having finished closely examining the wall around the outside door; it only took a few steps for him to reach my find. "Would you look at that! This place is just full of surprises," he said. He looked closely at the button then looked at me. I shrugged my shoulders. I was trying to mind what he said and not plunge ahead and maybe mess up a clue. He extended his glove-covered finger, took a deep breath and pushed. There was a click, and when he placed his hand on the smooth wall, a section started to swing forward, exposing another dark cavity.

Ash used his flashlight to add light to the newly discovered space. Despite his warning to me about going into strange places, he took a step. "It's a closet," he said. "A pantry, maybe." He took another couple of steps. I didn't follow him, but I did look through the opening and agreed. It was a comparatively small space, nothing like the room we'd found leading from the stylish library. Shelves held cans and boxes and pots and pans. Light filtered around the edges of another door that wasn't shut all the way.

He pushed the second door open. "This is a closet in the kitchen," he said. "It's a way to get to and from the library from the back of the house."

"I've been wondering about that," I said. "About how Miss Saint Pierre got into the library herself without leaving footprints in the living room carpet."

"Now we know," Asher said. "She must have come this way. She could have come down the staircase and gone into the kitchen to make herself a cup of coffee then gone into the library by way of this hidden passage. There was a cup on her desk containing a bit of what was probably coffee. That would have been handier than going around through the parlor." He grinned at me. "You aren't the only person who didn't notice that the carpet hadn't been walked on and wonder how either Miss Saint Pierre or the murderer got into the library. No one else did either." He returned to the room we'd been exploring when I'd found this secret way to the kitchen. "By the time everybody had put their prints all over the place, the clue was gone." He grinned at me. "But your mind noticed, stored it away for later, and recalled it today. Good work!"

As we returned to exploring the room we'd found, my mind was trying to absorb all the surprises we'd discovered. Mystery upon mystery was piling on. What would be next? It was too much for me to process at one time. I needed time to think about all the hidden doors and passageways.

"When this place was built, rumor says the earliest version of Briarwood became headquarters for a local bootlegging operation," Asher said. "That makes sense now that I see all this. It's why there are so many hidden places. Some were for hiding booze, while others were for hiding from the police if they were raided. Chances are we'll find more before we're through." He looked around the room. "This room probably was a storage room for illegal liquor. They could load it directly to a vehicle through the outside door," he gestured toward the ivy-draped opening, "and the other doors make it easily accessible from other parts of the house. In those days, there wouldn't have been any furniture in it. Miss Saint Pierre put a desk and chair, the barest of furniture, in it when she furnished the place. I doubt she actually used it for writing her books. I'm guessing that she might have just done that to show off."

As we continued our search of the newly found room, my mind continued to mull over the questions about the space. Why would somebody, even flamboyant LaRue Saint Pierre, put what looked to be a valuable carpet where it would be seen only by a limited amount of people? What purpose would it serve, except to cover the hardwood flooring? To muffle footsteps? Perhaps. Or maybe Ash was correct. She furnished it to show off her secret writing room. Maybe she planned to publicize it, like a gimmick. *Best-selling Author's Hidden Writing Room.* Or maybe there were more secrets to be discovered. As my mind wrestled with the conundrum, I thought back to earlier, when I was looking at the replica of the book cover. Between Ash and myself, we had studied just about every inch of the walls enclosing the small room. What else was there? I started walking. Using the wide border on the rug, around I went. When I got to my starting point, I moved to just inside the band of ornate design and did the same thing. When I started around for the third time, something felt different underneath my foot. I stopped and shifted my weight from one foot to another. There! A tiny squeak sounded, so faint that I wouldn't have noticed it if I hadn't been listening for a signal, a sign that something was there under the carpet.

Asher had started out the opening into the library when I stopped him. "I could use your help!" I called out, and he turned back. "Give me a hand with this carpet," I said.

He raised his eyebrows but didn't say anything. He grabbed the nearest corner of the floor covering and lifted it. I took the other corner at that end of the room and we began to roll the heavy carpet into a coil. After a couple of feet, my suspicion was proven correct. There was an area where it was obvious that the wooden flooring had been cut, forming an easily recognizable rectangle section. At the far end, a sort of strap made of heavy, flat canvas formed a handhold.

Ash gave a long, low whistle. "I'm going to start taking you with me to crime scenes," he said. "Just to find things other people miss."

CHAPTER FIFTEEN

He leaned over and grasped the loop. When he tugged, the wooden section at first appeared to be stuck, but when he pulled harder, the panel gave way with a screech. When it was all the way up, Ash peered into the opening, and I moved to stand by him. I saw nothing but blackness.

Ash turned his flashlight toward the gaping cavity, but the beam of light only illuminated the wooden steps leading downward into what appeared to be an empty space. "Stay here," he commanded, and this time I was only too happy to obey. I wasn't about to go down those steps into the darkness. Who knew what it held? Spiders, maybe. Spiders were one of my top fears, and I was only too happy to follow his order, especially since it cast me as an obedient observer rather than a wimp. Besides, it might be dirty and cobwebby down there. Hidden rooms were interesting. Holes in the floor were different. No thanks. I'd stay topside.

I saw the beam of light flashing around what looked as if it were an empty room, and sure enough, Ash verified that supposition when he came back up the steps.

"Nothing down there," he reported, "except cobwebs and dirt." He dusted himself off and poofs of powder flew from wherever his hands touched. It made me even happier that I hadn't followed him into the unknown. "It looks as if nobody has been down there in years. But," he looked at me and smiled, "good catch finding it. I might not have ever figured that out."

It was then that we heard voices coming from the other part of the house—the 'normal' part. The clean part. The part that until thirty minutes ago had been the only place we knew about. Now there were new secrets to puzzle over. New mysteries to solve.

The two men who walked into the library looked startled when Asher and I appeared from the gap in the bookshelves.

I recognized them as the policemen who had been present the day I'd found the body on the library floor.

"You're kidding!" one of them said. "We missed a whole room?"

"That's just a drop in the bucket," Ash said. "There's more, and we need anything and everything dusted for prints."

I had seen it all, and it was going to take time to introduce the forensic team to what we'd discovered. I just wanted to think about it, sort it out in my mind, so I went into the living room and took a seat on the sofa, trying to make sense of the new discoveries.

There had been no footprints on the carpet the day I found the body. How the murderer had come and gone had been solved when we found the section of shelving that was a secret door into a hidden room. Furthermore, how the killer had escaped without being seen was now explained by the door from that room to the outside, hidden by the curtain of ivy vines, although it was possible that the murderer had come and gone by the same path LaRue Saint Pierre had probably used, by way of the kitchen closet. The mystery of how LaRue Saint Pierre had gotten to the library without leaving footprints was solved when we found that secret passageway.

But the biggest mystery of all was why? Why would somebody want to kill LaRue Saint Pierre? Sure, her novels were what some people would call 'trash', but a lot of people enjoyed trash, I guess. She sure sold a lot of them. And even the most vocal critic of her novels wouldn't resort to murder to silence her, would they? If some nut had thought the world would be better without LaRue Saint Pierre and her books, wouldn't they be bragging about what they had done?

I was deep in thought when Asher came back into the room. "I'd better take you back to your office. The forensic team will be gathering new information for some time." I had hoped I could stick around longer, but I could see that there was nothing else to learn at this point. Any fingerprints they found would have to be compared to what was on file, and that would take a while.

When we were in Asher's car and on the way to my place of employment, he started cautioning me. "Don't tell anybody what we found today, Sissy. Not anyone. Understand?"

I just looked at him.

"Obviously, the killer was familiar with that room and the different ways to get in and out without being seen, and that's something few people would know." His eyebrows were raised as he looked at me to see if I really comprehended what he was saying and if I agreed. "It's very important that we keep this to ourselves." He kept looking my way, trying to judge my agreement. "If we let that bit of information get out to the public, we'll lose the advantage."

We pulled up to the front of the newspaper office, parking in the same no parking zone that he'd used earlier. "And that means your boss, Sissy. You, especially, should not tell Gene Hoskins about this. If he knew, he couldn't resist printing it."

"I promise," I said. "I won't tell him. I won't tell *anybody* at the paper." I put my hand on the door handle, in preparation for getting out of his car. "*If,*" I said, "you promise me that I'll get first notice when I can break the news to the public. As far as the *News* is concerned, this is *my* story." I was hoping he wouldn't notice my addition of the phrase 'at the paper', but, of course, that was too much to hope for.

"That's a deal," he said. "I won't give the story to anyone else, but I can't promise that for other people on the force. Sometimes things have a way of becoming public knowledge." He was staring out the windshield, and we both had the same thing in mind.

The car parked in front of us, in the first legal spot, was Miss Boo's Caddy. I owed a lot to Miss Boo. Like my job, and my apartment, and not ending up in the Biloxi jail, accused of murder. Miss Boo liked to be in the thick of things. She wanted to know what was going on in town. She liked to solve mysteries. I had no doubt that she was in the *News* office finding out everything she could about this blockbuster crime in her hometown. And she was waiting on me.

By now, she'd learned that I'd gone to the place of the crime with her grandson, and since she knew that it was unlikely that Ash would tell her anything, I was sure she was waiting to pump me for information.

"This is important, Sissy," Ash said, his voice firm. "This needs to be kept confidential. Don't tell anyone what we discovered today."

I hate to lie so I didn't answer.

"And tell Granny Boo the same thing when you tell her."

I grinned as I slid out the door. "Yes, sir. I will."

CHAPTER SIXTEEN

Miss Boo and my boss were standing near my desk when I walked in. "Here she is now," Gene Hoskins said. "Boo has come to take you for lunch," he said, and I knew he was angling for an invitation to join us. This happens frequently when she shows up around noon.

"I hear you've been going over the crime scene with my grandson," she said. *Please don't ask me if we discovered anything new.* I tried to send the message by way of telepathy, and it must have worked, because she didn't question me any further, but instead said something that surprised me.

"You've been spending too much time thinking about the murder, Sissy. Thinking about it and writing about it. It's time for you to put that aside. Let me take you to lunch and we'll talk about something else entirely.

"I've come by to ask for your help. I'm going to redecorate my dining room, and I can't decide what color and fabric to use for the drapes. And then there are the chairs. Should I reupholster or not? I have a stack of samples to go through as we eat."

That did away with any thoughts of sharing the newest discoveries at the crime scene with her. I shouldn't have worried. Miss Boo is adept at managing situations, and this was no exception.

"Gene, you can help decide." She sent an innocent smile his way. "I need a man's opinion. I don't know whether to go with brown or green as the primary color. And would pink be out of line as an accent color or would lavender be a better choice?"

Miss Boo is in command of all her faculties, and she knew just what would turn her wannabe suitor's thoughts away from lunching with the ladies. "No, thank you, Boo. I have some calls to make and errands I need to take care of. Maybe next time," he said, just as she'd planned. Miss Boo is nothing if not devious. "You ladies have fun."

"What if that hadn't worked?" I asked her as we walked away.

"I'd have had to add more to our plans," she said, giving me an innocent look. "We're going to eat in a little place over in Beeville," she said as we got into her car. "There's someone I want you to meet."

Really? She wasn't going to ask about what her hunky grandson and I were doing this morning? I waited in silence as she watched for a break in the traffic before pulling out.

"And you can tell me what you found out this morning. Whatever it was you didn't want to talk about in front of Gene."

I told her all about the secret room and the exit to outside, hidden by vines. "So that's how somebody got in to kill her!" she said.

"Probably, but there's more," I said and told her about the door into the kitchen by way of the pantry. "You can't tell anyone," I cautioned her. "It may be that the murderer is the only person who knows about the secret passages, and I promised Ash that you would be the only person I told, and that I'd caution you about letting the word out."

"I won't tell a soul," she agreed. "Not even Doris. Not until you tell me I can. I can understand why Asher did that—told you not to tell anybody. I imagine very few people know about that secret room, and one of them is the killer."

"And there's more," I said.

"More?" she said.

"More," I said, and told her about the trap door and the steps leading to a room underneath.

I had just finished telling her about all the secret passageways by the time we'd arrived in Beeville. Miss Boo pulled into the parking lot of The Hive, a cute little diner with yellow and black decor both inside and out. "We'll save talking about all that until we're alone," she said. "Now's the time for another approach, something else to wonder about. Doris and I ate here last week and enjoyed it. I think you will, too."

That stirred my curiosity. Another approach? Something else to wonder about? She had gone to the trouble of getting me out of the newspaper office without my boss for... what?

The waitresses at The Hive carried out the theme, all wearing black skirts or slacks with a white shirt, topped by a black apron with bees adorning it. The menu offered a light lunch, mostly salads, soups, and sandwiches, and we both ordered the special: a cup of soup and a scoop of chicken salad. The waitress took our order and had just walked away when the woman from the cash register approached us.

"Miss Boo, I'm happy you decided to visit us again."

"Vanessa, I enjoyed the meal I had last week so much that I just had to bring my friend, Sissy, to eat here. Sissy and I have traveled together, and she lives in my garage apartment. Vanessa owns this delightful place," she explained, and I thought she was being a bit much. "Traveled together" was a mild euphemism for finding a dead body and almost ending up in jail down on the Gulf Coast, and "delightful" wasn't a word I'd heard her use before. Not that it wasn't, but still, it was suspicious to hear her say that.

"I'm glad to meet you, Sissy. I hope you enjoy your lunch and come again. This is why we are growing. People enjoy our food and bring a friend."

Miss Boo spoke to me. "Sissy, Vanessa's grandmother taught at Mount Chapel High School and was my English teacher when I was in the eleventh and twelfth grades. She was *everybody's* English teacher, back in the day." She turned back toward the woman standing by our table. "Is she still doing well? Able to have visitors today?" Looking back at me, she explained, "Her grandmother is almost a hundred years old and lives in a retirement home. I visit her from time to time and reminisce."

"She loves visitors," Vanessa said. "She's still very alert and aware of what's going on in the world, and she loves to recall the past. She's told me how much she enjoys having you come to visit."

"I thought I'd take Sissy to meet her," Miss Boo said. "She's a reporter at the *Mount Chapel News*, and might like to hear what school was like back when I was a teenager. She writes special columns. One comparing high school fifty years ago with high school today would be interesting, don't you think?"

I hadn't thought of that, but it was a good idea. I'd have to run it by Gene Hoskins, but that sounded like something he'd go for. I doubted, however, that the subject of a then-and-now article was why Miss Boo had used subterfuge to spirit me away from the newspaper office to meet her elderly English teacher.

"She'd love to talk about that," Vanessa said. "And I'll send a cookie with you. That'll butter her up. She loves cookies from the Beehive."

When we went to pay our bill, Miss Boo added to her ticket. "I'd like six of those big chocolate chips cookies to go, please. I have a feeling my grandson is going to show up at my house any time now," she looked at me as she explained. "He loves homemade cookies, and I don't bake much anymore. But if he comes by, I can use these to bribe him for information."

Vanessa reached under the counter and pulled out a small box. "Here's one for my grandmother," she said as she put a large chocolate chip cookie in it. She took a larger box and used tongs to fill it with the cookies Miss Boo chose in addition to the chocolate chip variety she had already mentioned.

"So, what's up?" I asked my landlady when we got back into her car.

"You'll see," she said, playing it cagey. "I think you'll be very interested in what my high school English teacher has to say."

"Does it have anything to do with LaRue Saint Pierre and the mystery we're talking about?"

"Very much so!"

Five minutes later, we pulled up in front of a long, low building. The sign identified it as the Southern Pines Retirement Home. A manicured lawn was edged with low bushes, and a smooth walkway led to a wide porch furnished with comfortable looking chairs and small tables. It was a hot day, and nobody was taking advantage of the setting, opting to stay inside where the air-conditioning kept everyone cool.

When we entered the large front door, we were in a large, comfortable room furnished with sofas, chairs, and tables forming visiting groups. A woman, too young to be a resident, approached us. "Hello, Mrs. Bryce. It's good to see you again."

"Hello, Hailey. I've brought my friend, Sissy, to meet Mrs. Fewell. Sissy works at the *Mount Chapel News*. She's thinking about writing a piece about how different school is these days compared to when Mrs. Fewell taught."

"Glad to meet you, Sissy. I think you'll find her in the small visiting room down the hall." She gestured. "She'll enjoy the company. She likes to talk about the old days."

The excuse Miss Boo was using was beginning to sound authentic. I'd heard the saying, "If you tell a lie long enough it begins to sound like the truth," and it was proving to be true.

"Thank you, Hailey. We'll find her."

The elderly woman I met when we entered the small sitting room didn't look anywhere near a hundred years old. A small woman, she was neat and fashionable in a print dress, not a hair out of place, and appeared at least twenty years younger. She was watching a program about penguins on the big screen television when we got there.

"Emily!" she exclaimed when we entered. "What a pleasure to have you visit again." She picked up the remote and clicked the TV off. "They make the most interesting programs these days. They make learning actually fun. I wish they'd had programs like that back when I was teaching."

It took me a few seconds to remember that Miss Boo's real name was Emily. Of course, her old teacher would call her that instead of the nickname most people used these days. Depending on their age and how well they knew her, most people called her Miss Boo or just plain Boo.

"Here's something Vanessa sent you," Miss Boo said as she gave her the cookie from The Hive before strategically easing the conversation into the direction she had planned. "Sissy works at the *Mount Chapel News*. She's thinking about writing a story about school, then and now. I thought she should talk to you. If anyone remembers the students from past decades, it's a former English teacher."

That story was beginning to sound better every time she told it. I was starting to believe it myself, and ideas of what to include were popping inside my head. The introduction of the phrase "students from past decades" caught my ear. Where, indeed, was this going?

Mrs. Fewell was only too happy to expound on the subject, and I let Miss Boo guide the conversation. After a few minutes of discussion on the things that took precedence in teenagers' lives these days, Miss Boo turned the subject to the direction she intended.

"Mrs. Fewell had Lorraine Coggins in her class for Junior and Senior English," she informed me. Turning back to her former teacher, she asked, "Would you have thought she would turn out to be a famous author?"

An inelegant snort came from the refined woman. "I can't fathom it," she said. "I won't say that I don't believe it, but . . . ." She let the statement trail off. After a prolonged pause, she continued, "Her siblings were all adequate, a couple of them were A students in my class, and I could imagine them writing novels, but not Lorraine."

We sat in silence. Was that all she was going to say? I looked at Miss Boo and she returned my gaze, raising her eyebrows and giving me a small nod—my signal to take over the conversation. "She didn't do well in your class?" I asked.

"She flunked it," she said. "Badly. Then she went to summer school and scraped by with a low D. I gave her that D so she wouldn't have to do it all over again. It would have been useless. She couldn't do it, and she didn't care to learn."

"Then it must be a surprise to find out that she writes books," Miss Boo said. "Lots of books. Books that sell."

"Emily, if it was anyone else but you telling me that, I'd say they were lying."

Just then, a nurse came into the room. "Mrs. Fewell, it's time for your exercises," she announced.

"They have me exercising every day. They say it will keep me up and going." She stood and reached for an ornate cane that was leaning against her chair.

"Then we'd better go," Miss Boo said. "It's been so nice visiting with you. It brings back memories of high school."

"Same here. Come see me anytime," Mrs. Fewell said. "You too, Sissy. Anytime you want to talk about the old days in school, or anything else, for that matter, come visit. I like to talk," she said, her eyes twinkling with humor. "And I've heard everything the people here in Southern Pines have to say, and they've heard mine. Their stories are getting old." She chuckled. "I'm ready for some new ones."

We waited until we were in the car before either of us spoke. "Are you thinking what I'm thinking?" Miss Boo asked. I just looked at her, hesitant to say aloud what was bouncing around in my head, growing by the minute.

"Lorraine Coggins didn't write those books. Somebody else is LaRue Saint Pierre. Milton, most likely, however unlikely that might seem," she said.

As the elderly teacher spoke, those had been my thoughts also. But how did that work? And did that have anything to do with her murder?

When Miss Boo dropped me off at the newspaper office, I was afraid Gene Hoskins was going to have words with me for taking two hours for lunch. If we had spent the time talking about redecorating her dining room, my long lunch was out of bounds, and I couldn't mention what we were really doing without going against Asher's instructions about keeping things under wraps lest the murderer would know what we had discovered.

I was lucky. When I settled myself at my desk and looked around, I found that my boss had left the office. If my luck held, he wouldn't be back before quitting time. About an hour later, Miss Boo called.

"Come over for dinner. We have things to discuss," she said and hung up.

Indeed, we did have things to talk about. My mind was swirling with even more of the mystery. If Lorraine didn't write the books attributed to her, then who did? And why was she claiming credit? Or was she, really?

When my boss returned an hour later, I was answering and transferring calls, giving no clue that I'd taken an extra-long lunch break. I saw him look my direction, and I took care to look busy doing my job.

CHAPTER SEVENTEEN

It was a demanding week at the *Mount Chapel News*. When the notice spread about the murder of LaRue Saint Pierre, we were at the center of a firestorm. The article I'd written about finding the body spread all over the country, although my identity as Cecelia Townley, reporter, as opposed to Sissy Townley, receptionist, remained unconnected.

I was kept busy answering questions and transferring calls. Gradually, at first, then more rapidly, the town filled with strangers. There were reporters from all over the country, here to poke into every detail of the death of hometown girl Lorraine Coggins and her flamboyant alter-ego, novelist LaRue Saint Pierre.

Several of her siblings and cousins still lived in the vicinity, and they gained mild recognition from press and television. The murder of a famous relative was the most exciting thing that had ever happened to them, and it was also the most newsworthy occurrence to take place in Mount Chapel. When it was announced that she would be buried in a local cemetery, the crowds increased, eager to view the body at the funeral home and to attend the services at the church. Hopefully, there would be celebrities attending the funeral. Movie stars, perhaps, and other well-known authors.

With some thought and planning, it was determined that Lorraine, aka LaRue, would be buried near her parents and grandparents in the Eternal Peace Cemetery. The funeral home, Mortimer and Sons (slogan: *Sleep Quietly With Us*), finally had to keep their doors locked to prevent curiosity seekers from entering and searching the premises for the famed author's body. In the early days, a few people got in and were caught wandering around in places they should not have been. A former employee was arrested and thrown in jail for selling the security code to gain access to the building when it was locked, so it had to be changed. The judge ruled he had to stay in jail until after the funeral and interment. That was a new word for me—'interment,' which is a fancier way of saying the word most folks around Mount Chapel use, 'burial'. We're classier than that at the *News*, or want readers to think we are, so we use 'interment' in the paper.

The service was scheduled for ten days after Lorraine's death, allowing time for her relatives to travel to Mississippi from around the country. Cousins who never met her, or even cared about that branch of the family, were suddenly coming to cash in on the notoriety thrust upon the Coggins's clan. Relatives who had probably never even met the famous author were giving interviews to reporters from New York to California. "She had such talent as a child. I always knew she would be famous someday," one was quoted as saying.

Michael Mortimer Junior, in cooperation with Reverend Sylvester Lovejoy, pastor of the Last Chance Interdenominational Church of Forgiveness and Deliverance, which could hold more mourners than any other building in town, announced the funeral service would be held there and would be by invitation only. Other churches that wished to participate could do so, but without the presence of Miss Saint Pierre, and they could set their own rules as to who could come and who could participate. This led to several religious groups announcing special services that would take place at the same hour, and those who would preach against the sin and godless behavior that was espoused in Miss Saint Pierre's books.

Mount Chapel quickly filled with television cameras, newspaper and TV reporters, fans of LaRue Saint Pierre, and curiosity seekers. Locals and out-of-towners alike sold curios on street corners. The police ran them off, but they simply moved to another spot. The two motels in town (Shady Nook Courts and Happy Home Motel) as well as the Halfway Courts, which was between Mount

Chapel and Beeville, were soon jam-packed, and the spillover filled the hotels, motels, tourist courts, and bed and breakfasts in nearby towns. Everyone agreed that it was disagreeable and messy but excellent for the economy of Mount Chapel and the surrounding area. The shop keepers liked the money, but were ready for the hullabaloo to be over.

My boss decided to join the hubbub. He put everyone to work producing a special edition of the *News*. It was devoted entirely to LaRue Saint Pierre, her history in the time she lived here, complete with pictures of the schools she attended, her pictures through the years as found in the high school yearbooks, and her accomplishments, which weren't many.

The sports reporter was sent out to interview Lorraine's school friends, the ones he could locate, since most of them had moved away. It was assumed all her old teachers were long since deceased. Mrs. Fewell was not mentioned.

The advertising department had an easy time financing the extra edition of the paper. This issue would be a collector's copy, they were sure, and everybody would want one, not only locals, but people all over the country who were fans of LaRue Saint Pierre's books. Every business in town wanted their name prominently displayed. Gene was raking in the money and had hopes of keeping some of the advertisers when all the hoopla blew over.

The first printing sold out immediately, and Gene ordered another run. Memorabilia collectors snapped them up, betting they would become valuable in the not-far-off future.

It was a busy week for me as well. I worked long hours at the paper, but I didn't mind. It was interesting, and I met lots of people, both in print media, which I learned meant newspapers as well as books, and television folks too.

One day at the beginning of all this, Gene was staring at me, looking at me up and down. I wondered if I had done something wrong when he said, "Sissy, I don't know if you want all these people who are coming in and out of the office to know that you are the person who found Miss Saint Pierre's body."

I hadn't thought about that, but it was getting crazy around town, and what he said hit home. "No, I don't think I do," I answered.

"I'd just as soon keep you to ourselves," he said. "All the information you are privy to belongs to the paper."

"Yes, sir." I knew that. He had been adamant about protecting any information I came up with.

"Maybe you'd like to change your badge," he suggested. "So folks wouldn't recognize you as the author of the articles."

He was right about that, so I unfastened my pin-on identity and slipped it off. I was lucky that nobody so far had recognized me as the person who'd discovered the body nor as the person who'd written about it for the *News,* and I wanted to keep it that way.

"I'll have Mrs. Frewer make you a new one," he said. "Let her know what to put on it."

There wasn't a lot to choose from, but since my real name, Cecelia Townley, was the byline the readers and strangers knew me by, I decided Sissy, with no last name, would be sufficient, at least until all the publicity died down. I asked Mrs. Frewer to put that on my new badge. When she returned, I had a new name tag announcing me as "Sissy-Receptionist".

I wrote some shorter articles for the special edition of the paper, and for those I used my 'formal' name. I used the same private office I did when I wrote the original report of her murder. It was as if I were two separate people: Cecelia Townley, reporter, and Sissy Unknown, receptionist.

Miss Boo and I had conferred early on about the suspicion that someone other than Lorraine Coggins had written the books attributed to LaRue Saint Pierre, but we hadn't spoken of it since the visit with Mrs. Fewell and hearing her take on Lorraine's lack of ability to write a sellable novel. Although that interesting premise popped in and out of my head, I didn't have time to spend thinking about it. Most days, I worked late and picked up a hamburger and fries for supper on the way home. The few times Miss Boo and I met coming and going, she acted very mysterious. She wasn't as effusive as she usually was, as if she were holding something back. It wasn't until after the funeral that we had time to revisit the identity of LaRue Saint Pierre.

CHAPTER EIGHTEEN

After the funeral and all the "memorial" and "redemption" services had ended, Mount Chapel began to return to normal. The strangers who'd flooded the town went back to where they'd come from, or most of them, anyway. My job got back to just being a receptionist—directing phone calls and people from my position behind the front desk. It was still busy, just not as exciting as it had been recently.

One day about a week after all the services revolving around the murder of LaRue Saint Pierre had ended, Miss Boo showed up. "I've come to take you to lunch," she announced.

"I don't know, Miss Boo," I said. "It's been kind of busy. Mr. Hoskins might want me to stay here." At that, my boss walked up, as he always did when he saw my landlady come in the *News* office.

"Hi there, Boo," he greeted her. "Come to take Sissy to lunch, have you?"

"Yes, Gene, I have," she answered. "I'd invite you to go along except I also want to take her to meet somebody and hear about what might be the core of a very important story. One that will put our local newspaper back on the national scene when it breaks."

She had my attention, and Mr. Hoskins eyebrows went up. He questioned without saying a word.

"I don't want to tell you anything about it yet, just in case it turns out to be nothing. However, if it turns out the way I suspect it will, it'll be another scoop for Sissy. One that newspapers all over the country will be scrambling for. I'd prefer that we keep it close to the vest, as the saying goes, until we check it out."

"If you say so, Boo. If you say so! As long as the *News* gets first chance."

"Oh, it will, Gene! It will! You'll be the first to know. But not today. Today is for exploring the evidence," Miss Boo replied. "Getting to the root of the mystery."

"Then go on, Sissy," my boss said. "Boo has a way of knowing where the secrets are buried. Take all the time you need." On his way to his office, where his receptionist guarded the door from her own desk, he looked back at us. The expression on his face told me he was speculating about what we might be up to. I was wondering the same thing myself.

"Was that true?" I asked Miss Boo as we walked out the door.

"It was," she replied. "I wouldn't lie, now, would I?" Her eyebrows were arched high as she said that, and I couldn't tell if she meant that facetiously or not.

"No," I said, but I'm sure that doubt showed in my voice. There wasn't much doubt about where we were going when we took the highway toward Beeville, and she explained it by what she told me next.

"When we visited Mrs. Fewell that first time if you remember, she was adamant that Lorraine Coggins could not possibly have written the books that have been published under the name LaRue Saint Pierre. I could've just accepted or rejected the notion, but I didn't. The opinion could have been just a faulty memory of someone almost a hundred years old. I wanted more proof. More reasons as to why she thought that way. That would be something, wouldn't it? If Lorraine didn't write those books?" She glanced my way as she drove. I didn't answer. I knew she would expound on the idea.

"So, the next day I went to the Book Nook and bought a copy of every book they had in stock by LaRue Saint Pierre, whoever she might turn out to be," she continued. "Since the news of the murder had reached the public, her books were already selling fast. It was as if everybody in Mount Chapel had to have a copy just to see what all the hoopla was about, but I got several titles before they sold out. To tell the truth, I bought two copies of each. One for me and one to take to Mrs. Fewell."

"Okay," I said, not really understanding where this conversation was going.

"The next day I took the books to the retirement home. Today," she glanced my way, "we're going to see what she has to say about them."

"Oh!" I hadn't thought about that before. "That ought to be interesting," I said, although I didn't know that anything could be gained by the elderly English teacher giving her judgement about the romance novels. Thought-provoking, maybe, but how could her opinion about the writing have anything to do with solving the crime?

"I know," Miss Boo said as she pulled into a parking spot at the Southern Pines Retirement Home. "She might not have anything more than an opinion about the quality of the writing, but maybe . . ." She switched the key to off and looked at me. "She might surprise us."

The elderly English teacher was in her room, settled in a comfy arm chair. A window overlooked what appeared to be the remains of a flower garden, sunshine sending beams into her room. She was—what else—reading a book, which she lowered as we entered.

"Emily! It's good to see you!" she said. "I've been thinking that I needed to thank you for the pleasure you brought me." She raised the novel she was reading. "Not only me but other folks here in the home." She grinned. "I've been telling people that I taught the author of these novels how to write, and that gets a big reaction from everyone, given the details in some of them." Chuckling, she continued. "If they choose to believe that includes the subject matter, that's their mistake. It's made me a celebrity, at least here at Southern Pines."

"Given that Lorraine Coggins is the person who claimed credit for them, and you taught her all she knew about writing, you deserve that notoriety," Miss Boo said. She looked around for a chair to settle in for the crux of the conversation.

"Sit, Emily, sit," Mrs. Fewell said. "You, too, Miss . . . I'm sorry, I've forgotten your name."

"Cecelia," I replied, "but most people call me Sissy."

"You had a little brother, I warrant, or perhaps a sister."

"Brother," I replied as I pulled a chair closer. I didn't want to miss a bit of this conversation. Her comment about my name indicated that despite her advanced age she was still sharp as to the meaning and usage of words.

"I won't beat around the bush," Miss Boo said. "When Sissy and I were here a few weeks ago, you said that Lorraine Coggins couldn't possibly have written the best-selling books that are attributed to her. Now, after reading several of them, is that still your opinion?"

Mrs. Fewell's eyeglasses had slipped a bit, and she looked at Miss Boo over the top of them when she spoke. "Yes, that's still my judgement," she said, her voice firm. "But I can tell you who did."

CHAPTER NINETEEN

Miss Boo and I froze. I'm sure my mouth was hanging open. How? Who? Why?

Mrs. Fewell knew she had us enthralled with that statement. With the smallest of smiles, she looked from one of us to the other. All sorts of questions were running through my mind, but the biggest one was, "Is this old lady sharp enough to know what she's saying? Or does her age cloud her judgement?"

Miss Boo asked the question we were both thinking. "Then who did write them?"

"Lorraine's brother, Milton."

That makes sense, I thought, alternating with, *how could she know that?* I knew that Milton was his sister's . . .secretary? Right hand man? Facilitator? But the actual author of the books attributed to LaRue Saint Pierre? Weren't LaRue Saint Pierre and Lorraine Coggins the same person?

After sitting in silence for a few seconds, letting that information sink in, Miss Boo asked, "What makes you think that Milton wrote them?"

"As I told you when you visited earlier," Mrs. Fewell said, adjusting herself in her chair. She picked up a small pillow and put it to the small of her back, as if settling in for a long visit, "I was quite convinced that Lorraine had not written any novels. She couldn't write anything above a D-level back then, and it was inconceivable that she could improve that much in the intervening years, or even be interested in doing so. But. . . ." She broke off and reached for the glass of water on the table beside her.

Miss Boo and I were on the edge of our seats as we waited for further information. After taking a sip, Mrs. Fewell continued, "But she would be all too interested in being the persona she reflected as LaRue Saint Pierre. In high school, Lorraine was active in the drama club, and she was adept at playing the characters who were as flamboyant as the one she shows. . . er . . . *showed* to the public as the author of those novels. On the other hand, her brother, Milton, was an excellent writer. He usually got A's on his writing assignments. His short stories were excellent. Interesting. Well written except for certain phrases and words that he used incorrectly even after I'd corrected them repeatedly." She looked over the top of her glasses, from one of us to the other.

"Incorrectly?" Miss Boo questioned. "Can you explain what you mean by using words incorrectly?"

"They are phrases that are common—we hear them every day—but sometimes people say them incorrectly. Perhaps because they hear someone else saying it wrong, then they repeat it like that and never stop to think that it doesn't make sense. So, it gets passed along, and people don't give it any thought. Except for English teachers. We recognize it and don't like it."

"Can you give us an example?" Miss Boo asked, frowning. "I don't know that I fully understand what you mean."

"A common expression is 'one and the same.' Many people, including Milton, say or write 'one *in* the same.' No matter how many times I corrected him, he still wrote *in* instead of *and*."

"I know what you mean," I said. "I hear people saying 'to all *intensive* purposes,' when what they mean is 'to all *intents* and purposes.' It makes me grit my teeth. I want to correct them, but I just let it go by."

"Exactly," Mrs. Fewell said. "And I've reached the time of life when I can be a persnickety old woman and get by with correcting people. The other day I overheard one of the staff say 'You have to be *pacific* when you explain it.' I probably should have held my tongue, but I didn't. I said, 'You mean he needs to be *specific*, and she said, 'Isn't that what I said?' 'You said *pacific*,' I told her, and 'Pacific is the ocean on the west coast, among other things, such as peaceful. But 'pacific' and 'specific' are two different words with two different meanings.' I don't know if she understood what I was saying or not.

"Back when I was teaching," she continued, "I corrected my students when they said something incorrectly but not my friends and acquaintances. Not if I wanted to keep them as friends. But now that I'm old, I can correct people and get away with it." She chuckled.

"There are certain phrases that one hears in particular areas of the country. Authors who are from New England use words and idioms that aren't heard in other parts of the country, as do writers from the Midwest, or Texas, for example. There are phrases that we use here in southern Mississippi, ones that are sprinkled throughout the novels attributed to Miss Saint Pierre, that are technically correct—that is, phrases which are written and spelled the way they are intended, as jargon, but there are others . . ." She shook her head. "When I was reading the books that you brought me, whenever I came to one of those phrases, my mind immediately jumped to Milton, and I remembered correcting him." She shook her head. "But Milton just couldn't, or wouldn't, wrap his head around the correct usage of some of the words and phrases he used, and whenever I came across one in one of the books you brought me, I knew that he'd written it."

"When I was reading one of the LaRue Saint Pierre books and came across something like that, something that stood out, I just thought it was something Lorraine had used incorrectly, but you're saying it wasn't Lorraine doing it?" Miss Boo asked.

"If I thought Lorraine was capable of writing those books, that's what I might have thought as well," Mrs. Fewell said. "But she wasn't, so I didn't. No, I think Milton wrote those books. Milton is LaRue Saint Pierre."

"It looks like the publisher would correct mistakes like that," I said. "Don't they edit what the writer sends them?"

"I would think so," Mrs. Fewell said. "But judging from these books," she waved her hand toward the stack of books on the windowsill, "evidently not."

"Perhaps they thought they were just southern expressions," Miss Boo said. "The big publishing companies are mostly in New York, not here in Mississippi."

"Possibly," Mrs. Fewell said, but her voice sounded doubtful.

"It makes sense," Miss Boo said later, when we were on our way home. "The fact that Lorraine didn't really write the books might have something to do with the murder, but that doesn't help in figuring out who did it. Surely Milton wouldn't have killed her, especially if he was the person who really wrote them. He wouldn't want LaRue Saint Pierre to die. She was his source of income."

"I can guess at the purpose for Lorraine pretending to be LaRue," I said. "I imagine that the kind of novels we're talking about wouldn't sell as well if a man was credited with writing them, so Lorraine became the public image of the author while Milton actually wrote the books."

"You're right about Lorraine embodying the character of LaRue perfectly," Miss Boo agreed. "She had the appearance and personality for it. She was the three B's—big, blonde, and busty, like the characters in the books, and she didn't mind calling attention to herself."

"But without Lorraine, there would be no more LaRue Saint Pierre to write the books," I said. "She had positioned herself firmly in the public eye as LaRue."

"And that would mean no more money for Milton, wouldn't it?" Miss Boo mused. "I wonder what will happen now, as far as any new books are concerned?"

"I'm sure the LaRue Saint Pierre books make—or at least have made—a lot of money for the publisher. Do you think they know that Lorraine didn't write them? They can't very well come up with another LaRue, can they?"

"It doesn't look like they could," Miss Boo agreed, "But who knows? They do all sorts of shenanigans in the publishing business. I remember something similar happening a few years ago. I think the original author died and they just announced that somebody else would be writing the books under that name."

"Did it work?" I asked.

"I guess it did. I didn't read them. They really weren't my cup of tea, so I don't know if that was successful or not." She glanced my way. "I wouldn't be reading the LaRue Saint Pierre books either if it weren't for the mystery surrounding her death."

When we reached the newspaper office, Miss Boo pulled up in front but made no effort to park. When I opened the door to get out, she cautioned me. "Let's not tell anybody about this. I want to think about it a while."

"I won't," I agreed. "It's better that this idea stays private for now."

I went to my desk as soon as I entered the building. It only took about two minutes for my boss to show up at my side.

"Did you find out anything new?" he asked.

"We did," I said. "It's not anything I can talk about yet, but it's big. Very big." I considered the fact that Lorraine Coggins didn't write the novels attributed to LaRue Saint Pierre to be very big news, but does it have anything to do with her murder? "I can't talk about it yet," I repeated.

"But when you can, you'll write it up for the *News*, right?"

"Right. I have to figure out some things first, get all the facts right. When I do, I'll write it up. As long as I get a byline for it," I added. It occurred to me that I was beginning to be quite mercenary about my job. As long as I was doing the detective work, I wanted the credit. Not that I was the only person following leads, since Miss Boo was the person who'd found this source of information and shared it with me.

"Sure, Sissy! Of course you'll get the byline. I wouldn't think about giving the story to anyone else." He nodded his head, emphasizing his statement. "Just let me know when you're ready so I can leave room for it," he said then turned to go back to his desk.

I'd been dealing with phone calls and messages for about an hour when Miss Boo called. "We need to talk about this," she said. "Come for dinner. I'll take a casserole out of the freezer and put it in the oven and make a salad. Just us, so we can talk."

"Okay," I replied. "I'll stop and get something for dessert on my way."

"That sounds good," she replied and hung up.

CHAPTER TWENTY

A couple of hours later, I entered Miss Boo's kitchen; Larry woke long enough to see who'd arrived and, seeing a familiar face, he gave a couple of half-hearted thumps of his tail and went back to sleep. No danger. No treats. Nothing to get excited about.

"Lemon meringue," I said as I put the box on the counter.

"I'm glad you're here," she said. "I need to get a dish off the top shelf, and I didn't want to climb without someone to hold this firm." She pushed a three-step ladder to where she wanted it. "Just hold it steady so it doesn't move and throw me off."

"Let me get it, Miss Boo," I said.

"No, Sissy. I'll do it. I know which one I want." She'd already started up, so I took hold and held the steps firm. "Doris called and invited me to her house to eat, but I told her I couldn't—not tonight. I hope I didn't hurt her feelings." She reached the top and opened the cabinet door. "I think we ought to keep what we learned today a secret," she said as she pulled a dish from the top shelf. "I have a feeling that we're close to the information that's the key to who killed Lorraine and why, but we need to keep it to ourselves until we figure it out."

"And just who is it that you think committed the murder?" a masculine voice boomed. "And what makes you think that you can figure it out, and if you do, what happens when they come after you as well?"

I was startled but had the presence of mind enough to reach one hand out toward Miss Boo, who'd jerked in surprise and grasped the cabinet for support before turning toward the speaker. I didn't want her falling. She grasped the cabinet door tightly and came down a step, one hand clutching the serving dish she'd retrieved.

"Oh, hello, Ash," she greeted her grandson as if his sudden appearance was nothing out of the ordinary, which it wasn't, except that we'd been talking about something that we planned to keep a secret from him. "You're just in time for supper."

"I repeat," Asher said. "What makes you think that sticking your nose into this murder investigation won't bring the killer after you if he thinks you're on to him?"

"Asher, come help me down off this ladder while Sissy holds it steady," she said, ignoring his question. It was obvious—to me at least—that it was a move taken to get his attention off the conversation and onto her safety while she thought up an answer that didn't give away more information than she wanted to tell. He did as she asked, but the expression on his face reflected the fact he was still upset about what he'd overheard as he entered the kitchen.

As soon as Miss Boo's feet touched the floor, he went back to questioning her. "What are you two up to?" His grandmother took the dish she'd retrieved from the high cabinet to the sink, ignoring him, so he turned his attention toward me, but I wasn't about to answer. If we were in hot water, let Miss Boo explain. He wouldn't be nearly as upset at his grandmother as he would with me.

"Come on! I'm not going to let this drop, so one of you might as well answer now instead of me haranguing you all evening. That would spoil dinner for all of us, wouldn't it?" He looked at me as he asked the question, but I glanced away.

"We aren't doing anything dangerous, Ash. I promise," Miss Boo said.

"You don't know what danger is, Granny Boo. You were on top of a ladder, for heaven's sake."

"It's nothing like that at all, Asher," she said.

"Then tell me what it is," he said, his voice firm, like he was determined to have his question answered. "Tell me what you two have been doing," he repeated, and it was obvious he wasn't going to let the matter drop.

"Just talking to someone," his grandmother said.

"Who?"

"No one you know, Asher."

"Tell me," he said in a firm tone.

"If you must know . . ." she started, then paused.

"I do," he retorted, "I must know."

"My high school English teacher," Miss Boo said, and from the tone of her voice, I almost expected her to say "so there," the way bratty kids do.

She had a satisfied look on her face as she rinsed the retrieved dish and picked up a towel to dry it. Asher, on the other hand, looked confused. Whatever he'd expected, it wasn't that.

"Your high school teacher?" he repeated dubiously. "And he's still alive?"

"Don't be a smartass, Asher. Yes, *she's* still alive. I'm not *that* old."

"And what could *she* possibly say that would have any bearing on the murder?" His voice was still firm, and his scowl never wavered, his glare remaining firmly fixed on his grandmother. It was obvious he was not going to let the subject drop.

When Miss Boo didn't answer immediately, Asher turned his attention to me. "Cecelia?" I knew he was determined when he called me Cecelia instead of Sissy, but I wasn't about to let him start questioning me. I ducked my head and walked over to the dining table, wondering if I needed to make a trip to the bathroom. My desire to know the outcome of this contretemps was stronger than my wish to stay out of the line of fire. I didn't want to miss anything, so I stayed put.

"She said," Miss Boo saved me from his determined questioning. "She said that Lorraine didn't write those books—the ones by LaRue Saint Pierre."

Asher just stared at her. Whatever he'd expected her to say, it wasn't that. When he glanced back at me, I just shrugged my shoulders, and he went back to questioning Miss Boo. "And this is important, why?"

"Because Lorraine was getting fame and attention for being a well-known author, not to mention the money!" Miss Boo said, her voice exasperated. "And since the world thought Lorraine was LaRue Saint Pierre, the actual author wasn't. Getting the fame and money, that is. That could lead to some bad feelings." She went back to getting dinner on the table, slipping the aluminum pan of hot casserole into the dish she'd just retrieved from the high shelf. "Sort of like this dish," she said as she picked it up and moved it from the countertop to the table.

"Like the dish?" Ash asked, and the look on his face said he was becoming even more confused.

"Anyone who looked at this would think I made it and baked it in my own oven. It looks like I did. It's in my own container. But I didn't have a thing to do with it. I just warmed it up." She looked at Asher. "Understand?"

"Maybe," he said. "So, who wrote all those books?"

"Her brother, Milton."

"And he didn't take credit for them because . . .?"

"Because women don't buy that kind of book when it's written by a man," she answered firmly. "And he would probably have trouble even selling a publisher on the idea. But if they thought somebody like Lorraine Coggins wrote it, then. . . ." She shrugged her shoulders. "You have to admit, Lorraine embodies the characters that are portrayed in the novels by LaRue Saint Pierre." She pulled off the oven mitts and tossed them on the counter. "It's easy to imagine her as the heroine in any of them, and from there to author isn't much of a step. Nobody would imagine her brother as the author."

"And Milton could write?"

"Milton could write," she affirmed. "And our old English teacher verified that and more."

"What more?"

"Mistakes. Certain mistakes of word usage Milton always made back in high school are the same ones that are in the LaRue Saint Pierre books."

He still looked confused, and I didn't blame him. The whole case was getting more complicated, if that was even possible.

"But," Miss Boo said. "Milton wasn't being forced to write the books that Lorraine claimed were hers. He did it of his own free will, so I can't see any reason that he would kill her. Whatever his share of the profits he made, he must have been satisfied or he would have just stopped writing them."

"So, there's no motive for Milton to kill his sister," Asher said. "He doesn't gain anything from her death. He loses."

Miss Boo opened the refrigerator and removed a bowl of salad, putting it on the table. "Sit," she said, and we took our places. She said a brief blessing, a thanks to God for all we received, and we started serving our plates.

"And . . ." Asher muttered, and he trailed off.

"And what?" Miss Boo prodded when he didn't continue.

"I can't see that Milton would kill her. That cut off the source of income," Ash mused. "And with Lorraine, known to the public as LaRue Saint Pierre, dead, he couldn't suddenly announce that he was the author of all those books, could he?"

"I wouldn't think so," Miss Boo agreed.

"No, I can't imagine him doing that," Asher said. "Besides, we haven't found any sign of animosity between them."

"Remember, he came in that morning when I found her body, when the police were already there. I don't think he faked being surprised and upset," I reminded them.

"Nor do I," Miss Boo agreed. "He was genuinely upset."

We were all quiet, and as we ate, we sank deep into our thoughts, trying to reason who and why anybody would want Lorraine dead.

"So, who else, besides Milton and Lorraine, would have a stake in the success or failure of the LaRue Saint Pierre books?" he finally voiced the question that was on all our minds. None of us had the answer to that.

"Or maybe it's the other side of the coin," Miss Boo said. "Why would anyone who had a share of the income from the sale of LaRue Saint Pierre books kill the goose that supposedly laid the golden egg?"

CHAPTER TWENTY-ONE

"That's the question, isn't it?" Miss Boo mused. "Along with who knew the secret way to get in and out of the house."

"Exactly," Asher said as he reached for the serving spoon and ladled another pile of chicken and noodles onto his plate. "Or would even know about the arrangement between Lorraine and Milton." He reached for the salad tongs and helped himself to another pile of chopped fresh veggies. "Or what if . . ." He paused, staring off into space.

"What if what?" Miss Boo asked. "Finish your thought."

"I was going to say, what if it has nothing to do with books or writing."

"Like what?" I questioned.

"I don't know," he answered. "Something we haven't discovered yet."

The three of us sat without speaking as we tried to come up with any other motive for the crime.

"It obviously has to involve somebody who knows the way to get in and out," Miss Boo said.

"Any one of the workmen who were on the crew that remodeled the house for Lorraine probably knew about the secret rooms," I said, "and how to move around the house without being detected." I mulled over that thought, trying to come up with why some unknown workman would kill Lorraine. "But I can't think of why any of them would have a reason to kill her."

We were all lost in our thoughts, and several minutes passed before the conversation started again.

"Who publishes the books?" I asked. "What company? Would they know about any financial arrangement? Or for that matter," I paused as the train of thought grew, "would they even know that Lorraine wasn't really the author of all those books?"

Asher hesitated, a fork full of noodles halfway to his mouth. "How does publishing work?" he asked, looking back and forth between his grandmother and me.

"It's my understanding," Miss Boo said, "that an author can sign a contract with a publishing company, and that company produces the books either in printed form or as electronic books and sends a percentage of the income to the author." She rested her fork on the plate and put both hands on the table to push herself back. "Or the author can do it all themselves. But I don't think," she said as she stood up, "that Lorraine did that, whether she actually wrote them herself or not. All her books are for sale at the Book Nook, and I don't think self-published books are found anywhere but on the computer."

She held her index finger in the air as she said, "I'll be right back." Disappearing into the dining room, she returned quickly with a book in her hand. She took her seat again and opened the book cover that displayed a half-dressed, voluptuous woman looking sultry. "Here," she said, opening the first couple of pages and handing the book to Asher. "This is the publishing company and their address."

"May I borrow this book?" he asked his grandmother. "Just until I copy the address of the publisher."

"Yes, of course," she answered. "I have copies of several of her books."

"Are they all from the same publishing company?" her grandson asked.

"I don't know," Miss Boo answered. "I'd have to look." She picked up her fork and started eating again. "And I don't have them all. They were sold out of several titles when I bought those."

"This is enough to start," Asher said and went back to eating.

When we finished, including slices of the pie that I'd contributed to the gathering, we shared in clearing the table and getting the dirty dishes into the dishwasher. There was little conversation. There was a lot to think about, but not much anyone could add to what had already been said. It had been a long day, and I was ready to be home.

"I'll walk you home," Asher said as I slipped into my coat. "Just to be safe."

I hadn't felt unsafe until he added the "just to be safe" comment, but started rethinking the assumption that nothing bad could happen right outside my door. Not that I objected to the hunky policeman seeing me home. He had done it before, and the short trek often ended in a most satisfactory way, with a kiss that left me shivering and wanting more.

There was a different vibe tonight, though, and I felt safer having him by my side. There were flood lights set to come on when motion was detected, and they lit up the night as we stepped off Miss Boo's back porch. Another set, attached to the garage apartment where I lived, came on when we stepped through the gap in the hedge and into my yard. Instead of lingering at the foot of the steps as we had in the past, Asher said, "I'm going up with you." The tone of his voice did not indicate that he had any romantic intention when he said it, and that added to my feeling of unease.

When we reached the top of the steps, Asher one step lower than I was, he said, "Give me your key."

"Uh . . .it's not locked." Maybe I ought to rethink that habit.

He gave me an incredulous look that said, "Are you crazy?" without any words being spoken. He slid by me to open my door and enter first. As he brushed against me, I felt the gun in the holster. So that's why he hadn't removed his jacket during supper as he usually did. That made me even antsier. If Ash, who'd worked undercover in a biker gang, kept his gun close to hand, then he thought there was at least a possibility of danger.

The apartment over the garage, which hadn't held a car in years, even mine, consisted of two large rooms and a bathroom. The space we entered was comfortably furnished with a plump sofa, an inviting chair, a television set, and a small desk. On the far wall was a compact kitchen with a stove, fridge, and cabinets. A small table with chairs, one of which I moved to the desk when I worked there, separated the two spaces. A brief glance was all it took, since there was no place for anybody to hide. I had left a lamp on when I went to work that morning, as was my habit, and it kept the space well-lit.

There were two doors on the left wall. One led to the bedroom, the other to the large bathroom which also opened into the sleeping space. The bedroom door stood open, and Ash cautiously stepped in, looking around. I stood back a few steps. His caution was making me antsy. I didn't really think there would be anyone hiding in my bedroom, but still . . .. He opened the closet door, looked into the bathroom, and even bent and looked under the bed. I noticed that the whole time he kept his hand close to the gun under his jacket.

"All clear," he said.

"Didn't you expect it to be?" I questioned.

"Yes, but you can never be too careful."

I walked with him to my front door, and he glanced around before he stepped out onto the landing. "Keep this locked," he said firmly, turning the bolt so it would be secure automatically once it closed. "And fasten the chain as well."

"I always do," I said, somewhat peeved that he thought he had to tell me that.

"And check all your windows, be sure they're locked."

"Yes, sir." I glared at him.

"Until we catch whoever killed Lorraine, be extra diligent." His voice softened. "We have no idea what was behind the murder, and I don't want anyone who might think you know who did it coming after you. Understand?"

"I understand," I said, somewhat mollified by his concern. He leaned forward and gave me a peck on the lips. Not the kind of kiss I would have preferred, but it would have to do. For now.

CHAPTER TWENTY-TWO

The next morning when I woke up, I wondered why I'd been so spooked the night before. There was no one out to get me. Whoever murdered Lorraine Coggins didn't have it in for me, and the fact that her brother, Milton, might very well be the true author known as LaRue Saint Pierre had some bearing on the deductions that Miss Boo and I—with the help of the elderly teacher—had made, but I couldn't see how that would make me a target of whoever killed Lorraine. I just couldn't imagine why I would be in danger.

When I showered, I felt like I was washing away the ghosts of yesterday, and I arrived at work ready for another day of discoveries and surprises. It wasn't long before my boss strolled up to the reception desk that was my territory.

"Have anything new to write about today, Sissy?" he asked, obviously fishing for a clue as to what Miss Boo and I were about yesterday.

"Not yet, Mister Hoskins," I replied. "I'm working on something important, but I'd rather keep it under wraps for now." I felt like a real reporter, using a phrase like 'under wraps.'

"Of course. I understand." He nodded and started back to his office. He'd taken a few steps before turning to add, "Take all the time you need, and if you have to be gone . . ." he paused, "It's okay."

"Yes, sir. Thank you," I said. At least I had permission to take off if needed to work on the story, just like a real reporter. If I had any idea about what to write about, which at this point, I didn't.

My head was filled with ideas tumbling all over themselves with the new information, but I didn't know what to make of it. So what if Milton was the author of the sexy books that were attributed to his sister? I assumed they had some sort of arrangement about the money that came in from sales. Didn't her death cut off his source of income? I would think so. Because of that, if for no other reason, such as familial love or a sense of right and wrong, he wouldn't have killed her. Around and around the mystery circled in my brain, and I didn't know what the next step in solving the crime would be. I had no clue about how to find out about any contract between Lorraine and her brother. I wondered who and where her lawyer was, but even if I knew, he surely wouldn't share any information with me. It would take the police to inquire into any legal or financial arrangements Lorraine might have had. I thought about how I could take another step in solving the mystery. I pondered a lot of things that I didn't have a clue about.

But Miss Boo did. A day later, she showed up at my desk, unannounced, as usual.

"The plot thickens," she said. "Get your purse and tell Gene you have to go."

"Okay," I said. "Go where?"

"I'll explain in the car," she said.

My boss was approaching from the direction of his office.

"Boo, good to see you," he said.

"I've come to take Sissy again," she said. "There's been another development."

"Oh?"

"I can't tell you what it is," she said. "You'll know when it all comes together."

"All right," he said as he looked at her over the top of his glasses.

"It will be a big story when she writes it up."

He looked at me, and I nodded my head in agreement. It would certainly be a big story when it was announced that LaRue Saint Pierre was a man, not a woman, and even bigger if we could figure out who murdered the famous author, who wasn't even an author at all.

When we got in Miss Boo's car I asked, "So what's happened?"

"First thing this morning, I took Old Blue in for his regular service call." She patted the dashboard as she said that. "Old Blue" was Miss Boo's name for her car, an older Cadillac that she kept in tip-top form.

"Okay," I said, puzzled as to where this was leading that was important enough to come get me from my job.

"I was waiting in the service area when Tim Nowlin saw me. Tim is the man who sells me all my cars."

"Okay," I said again. Tim must not sell her many cars. She'd been driving the same car since I'd met her last year, and it was a few years old.

"Tim said, 'Mrs. Bryce, let me show you what I just got in the other day,' and since I'd forgotten to bring a book to read while I was waiting, and I was bored, I went with him to the showroom. Tim has been selling me my cars since day one, and he knows what I like, but he doesn't try to sell me. That is, he doesn't put pressure on me. He just shows me the latest thing in stock, and hopes I'll fall in love with it, and sometimes I do."

Surely she isn't taking me to see a car she's thinking about buying, I thought. Miss Boo is rich enough she can buy any car at the dealership. Heck, she could buy the whole dealership if she wanted to, and she doesn't need my opinion to choose a new vehicle. "Okay," I said again, beginning to sound like a broken record.

"And you'll never guess who was there, looking at cars." She gave me a sideways look, like she expected me to guess.

"Who?"

"Milton Coggins's wife. But you'd never recognize her now."

"Really? Wasn't she the short, mousy woman with frizzy brown hair who was with him at the funeral?"

"That was then. She's somebody else now." She hurried to explain. "Not really somebody else, but she *looks* like somebody else, like a whole new person. She has bleached blonde hair, about the same color as Lorraine had as LaRue. She was wearing skintight pants and a low-cut top, and she glittered."

"Glittered?"

"Glittered," she repeated. "Sparkled. She looked as if she was trying to become the image that Lorraine portrayed as LaRue Saint Pierre."

"Huh!" I couldn't think of anything to say as the image rolled around in my mind. "Trying to be LaRue," I repeated. "With the old LaRue dead, and Patricia's husband the actual author, they need a new LaRue Saint Pierre."

"Exactly!" Miss Boo said. "But that's not all."

I just looked at her, but I didn't ask. She'd tell me.

"There was somebody there with her. A man. And it wasn't Milton. He was good-looking. He had black hair and an olive complexion. He was Italian." She paused. "Or Spanish." After another pause, she added, "Or from some South American country."

She had my attention.

"He was looking at the cars on the showroom floor while she was talking with the salesman."

"Are you sure he was with her? Maybe he was just another customer in the showroom at the same time," I speculated.

"I thought about that," she said. "Really, I did. So when Tim walked me back to the service area waiting room, I asked him. 'Tim', I said. 'Who is that person with that blonde woman looking at cars?' and he said he'd find out for me. 'Be discreet, Tim', I said. 'Don't say I asked.' When he returned, he said it was the brother of the lady who was looking at the new Caddies."

"Her brother?" I repeated. "Milton's wife has a brother, and she's looking at new cars?"

"That's the story," she said.

"Maybe she needs a new car, or maybe he's the one car shopping, but she's asking the questions."

"Maybe."

We drove a bit further in silence.

"Now, I'm the one with questions," she said.

"And maybe there are some interesting answers," I replied.

"Exactly," Miss Boo said. She pulled the car into a driveway, and I looked around to see where we were. I'd been paying more attention to what Miss Boo was saying than to where she was going. The house we'd parked in front of was long and low, obviously very posh, in a neighborhood of similarly affluent homes.

"Where are we?" I asked.

"This is Milton's home," she said. "Milton and Patricia Coggins. We are making a condolence call. It was so hectic, you understand, that we put it off until all the ado settled down." She studied me for a moment then said, "Pull your name tag off, and leave it in the car." While I was unfastening the ID that proclaimed me to be '*Sissy-Receptionist-Mount Chapel News*' from my shirt, she reached in front of me and opened the glove box. She rummaged around in the clutter of papers and came up with a pair of glasses, black-rimmed and ugly. "Wear these," she directed. I wondered why we were altering my appearance, but I did as she asked. Not asked. Commanded.

When she opened her door and got out, I followed suit. Opening a rear door, she retrieved a bakery box from the back seat. "Come, come," she ordered and marched toward the front door. I didn't fully realize it then, but she was getting into character. I did as she asked. No, not asked. Instructed. Maybe even ordered. Obviously, Miss Boo had a plan in mind, and I was to follow her lead.

The doorbell played chimes that we could faintly hear through the ornately etched door and surrounding glass. A few seconds passed before it was opened by a smaller version of Lorraine Coggins. Or LaRue Saint Pierre. Or any of the characters from one of the books that were so famous.

She was shorter than I'd imagined Lorraine had been, but then I'd only seen Lorraine as a dead body on the floor. This woman was more petite, but other than that, a smaller version of a character from one of the famous books stood before us. Blonde hair, teased to outstanding proportions, surrounded her head. Her face, adorned with blush, eye shadow, and bright coral lipstick, reflected puzzlement at our appearance. Maybe she was wondering if we were there selling something, like door-to-door salesladies. Miss Boo rushed to explain our presence.

"Mrs. Coggins, my name is Emily Bryce, and this is my companion, Sissy."

I have to stop here and explain something. I met Miss Boo about a year ago when I gave her a ride to the Mississippi Gulf Coast, where I was headed to look for a job. Along the way, we'd found a lost dog that turned out to be the key to a drug-smuggling operation, we found a dead body and were almost arrested for the murder, and were ultimately rescued by Miss Boo's hunky policeman grandson, Asher Donovan. After all that, I thought of Miss Boo as an inimitable old lady, sort of my partner in crime, so to speak, and we were buddies. She talked me into abandoning the idea of finding a job down on the Gulf, where crime oozed out of every opportunity for employment or a career. Instead, I came back here to her hometown, and she got me a job at the local newspaper, the *Mount Chapel News*.

It took a while before I realized that the rest of the world, except for the citizens of Mount Chapel, Mississippi, had a different image of Miss Boo than I did. To most people, she was Emily Bryce, widow of the founder of Bryce Petroleum, which had sold to "big oil" for millions and millions of dollars. The whole Bryce family was wealthy. She was mother to a son, "Super" Bryce, who owned a large plantation in the next county and was rich all on his own initiative besides his share of the sale of Bryce Petroleum. She also had a daughter, Samantha Bryce Donovan, a well-known local attorney who was considering a run for state office in the next election. Samantha is Asher's mother. The name Bryce implied wealth and power to the rest of the county and the rest of the state. To the rest of the country, for that matter. To me and her friends, she might be Boo Bryce, but to strangers, she was Emily Bryce, of the oil company Bryces. She was the attorney's mother, the plantation owner's mother, and, above all, a society matriarch and cultural icon of Mount Chapel, Mississippi.

That day, when she came to the office to fetch me, she was Miss Boo. When we exited her car in front of the classy house and walked up the path to the front door, she magically became Mrs. Emily Bryce, of the Bryce Petroleum Bryces. And I was no longer Sissy Townley, receptionist-slash-reporter. Now I was partner in crime, so to speak, of whoever Miss Boo was that day. I was the assistant and flunky to the rich Mrs. Emily Bryce. I was unimportant. Inconsequential. No need to watch what you say in front of Sissy. She didn't matter. My job was to listen and observe.

I rarely saw this metamorphosis. I saw it when we checked into the expensive hotel down on the Gulf Coast. That Mrs. Emily Bryce had gotten us an elegant suite in a hotel that had no rooms available. Miss Boo was my friend. Mrs. Emily Bryce was out to get something. But what?

CHAPTER TWENTY-THREE

"I must apologize, Mrs. Coggins, for not having visited you earlier," Miss Boo, speaking as the rich Mrs. Emily Bryce, said. "Until the recent death of your sister-in-law, I had not realized that you and your husband had returned to Mount Chapel. I knew Milton many years ago, back when we were in school, but I hadn't seen him in ages. Of course, my last name wasn't Bryce back then. Our paths went in different directions. I married and had my own interests, while Milton went another way. We lost touch."

Not that the poor Coggins family would have been in the same circles of society as the Petroleum Bryces anyway, but the refined Mrs. Bryce wouldn't mention that.

"It is regrettable that it took a tragedy for old high school alumni to reconnect," she said.

It only took a beat for the stunned Mrs. Coggins to realize who was standing at her door. Even newcomers to Mount Chapel quickly learned that the Bryce family were high on the society A-list. Or would be if there was such a list. "Won't you come in, Mrs. Bryce?" She was flustered at the appearance of a total stranger, a rich and important stranger to boot, at her door but recovered quickly. It was a feather in her cap to have such a person come calling. "And . . ." She trailed off, not knowing what to do about me.

"Sissy, come along," Miss Boo commanded, as if I wouldn't have followed if she hadn't instructed me to do so. I would pretend I was Larry, not exactly a lap dog but a follower, not a leader. Not a person who made themselves known, but somebody who understood that their place in life was to follow, listen, and keep quiet. Miss Boo had cast me in this role, and I would follow her lead without question.

"Please accept this token," Miss Boo said as she handed over the bakery box. "I apologize for having purchased it rather than it being homemade, but I seldom cook, and I gave up having kitchen help long ago, except for special occasions." She thought about my presence and decided she had to give some explanation for why I was straggling along after her. "Of course, I have Sissy, and she accompanies me and helps me in myriad ways." She gave me a smile. "I feel more secure with a younger person nearby in case I need help."

That was laying it on thick. I was afraid she'd go too far in explaining why I was there, but before she could add more to her autobiography or mine, our hostess ushered us into the living room. When we were settled on the long, velvet covered sofa, Miss Boo shifted the conversation around to the subject she was aiming for.

"Patricia, it was upsetting to hear of your sister-in-law's death. Were you two close?"

"Call me Trish, please," the LaRue copy-cat said, frowning. "No, not really. Milton and I have only been married a few months, and his sister and I hadn't had the chance to get well acquainted yet. She was completely involved with her books, and I was busy settling in to life in Mississippi."

"How sad," Miss Boo said. "You seem like such a friendly person. I'm sure you and Lorraine would have become the best of friends over time."

"I *try* to be," the blonde simpered, immediately trying to curry favor with the rich and important Emily Bryce. "I *try* to get along with all my husband's family." The expression on her face and the tone of her voice didn't match the words coming out of her mouth, and the emphasis on the word "try" contradicted the impression she was attempting to give. It was obvious that she and Lorraine were not friends, despite the close relationship each of them had with Milton.

I could have told her why. The marriage of a man who was only a few years younger than Miss Boo and a woman young enough to be his daughter—or maybe even his granddaughter—brought all kinds of speculation about her motives. I'll bet Milton, being caught in the middle, had been pulled both ways.

"And you and Milton haven't been married all that long?" Miss Boo questioned.

"Not quite a year."

"Newlyweds!" Miss Boo exclaimed. "How exciting! Where did you meet?"

"In Vegas," Trish answered, looking at the large diamond ring on her finger, turning her hand this way and that while admiring the sparkle it gave off. She looked as if she were angling for a comment, but neither of us took the bait.

"In Las Vegas!" Miss Boo exclaimed. "Are you from there?"

"Originally, I was from Los Angeles, but I was working in Vegas and met Milton when he was there visiting."

"Your love story might be the plot for one of Lorraine's books," Miss Boo said. "It's too bad she died before she could write it."

Trish frowned. "Maybe . . . maybe she had. . ." she stumbled to a stop then looked up. "She had some books written when she died, so maybe that's one of them," she explained. "There will still be some LaRue Saint Pierre books released. Several, in fact."

Miss Boo didn't follow that line either, but pursued the path she had set. "And what did you do there, Trish? You are very attractive. Did you dance in one of the shows?"

"No, I didn't." She put a sad expression on her face. "Unfortunately, I broke my ankle when I was a child, and it left me unable to perform dance moves. It was just too painful. No, I wasn't a showgirl."

Miss Boo just sat there, nodding, but she didn't say a word. It worked. Thinking she had to add to that bit of information, Trish continued. "I had several jobs in Vegas. I worked in some of the big casinos, welcoming guests, introducing them to the various entertainments the city had to offer."

"How interesting," Miss Boo said. "Sort of a 'Welcome to Las Vegas' hostess."

"Yes, exactly," Trish said. She'd been edgy while trying to describe her occupation, but Miss Boo's words put her at ease. She smiled and relaxed. Personally, I wondered if she was describing a job as a hooker without using that word. Likely she was relating her occupation in more ladylike terms.

"It's been so nice getting to know you," Miss Boo said. "I'm sure we'll be seeing more of each other. I didn't know Lorraine as well as I did Milton. She was much younger, you know, which was more important when you're in high school but not so much as an adult."

"Well, she was older than I am," Trish said, scowling. "And showed it."

What a rude comment, I thought. It was obvious Trish didn't care much for Lorraine. Just because they were sisters-in-law didn't automatically make them friends, but I was surprised that she didn't try to hide it. I thought that most people would not be so obvious about their dislike of a relative, much less somebody who'd just been murdered. Miss Boo pushed the conversation in that direction.

"I imagine your sister-in-law stayed occupied with writing her books. Were you able to spend much time doing things together? Getting acquainted?"

Trish looked away. The look on her face said that she didn't have a very good opinion of the famous author. "She didn't want to get acquainted," she said. "She was too rich and famous to be friends with a poor unknown like me."

The animosity oozed out. It was apparent the two women weren't friends, but were they enemies? Maybe. Could she have been the person who did the dastardly deed? If she was, surely she would pretend to at least get along with Lorraine, even if she couldn't bring herself to claim a close friendship. I wondered if there was any way Asher could find out if she owned a gun, and if the bullets that killed Lorraine could be tested to determine what kind of gun they came from. I don't watch true crime shows much, but on TV, they can do that.

So many things were swirling around in my head that I lost track of the discussion until Miss Boo stood and made a motion with her hand to urge me up as well.

"I'm so happy to have made your acquaintance, Emily," Trish was saying when I tuned back in to the conversation. "Perhaps we can have lunch together some day. I've been urging Milton to join the Mount Chapel Country Club, and when he does, I'd love to take you to lunch there," she hinted. Giving me a weak smile, she added, "And your companion as well, of course."

"Trish, feel free to call me Mrs. Bryce," Miss Boo said in a sharp voice. That put a confused expression on Trish's face as she tried to figure out if the words were a reprimand or not. "We'd better be going now. Come along, Sissy." She walked briskly toward the front door. The tone in her voice when she informed the young woman how to address her elders told me all I needed to know about what she thought about Trish's manners.

"Well!" she said when we climbed into Miss Boo's car. She sat still, both hands on the steering wheel, and stared straight ahead. "Well!" she said again. Finally, she shook her head and started the motor. Backing into the street, she drove down the block before saying, "Well," for the third time. After a few seconds, she added, "I guess she didn't know that Lorraine had wanted to join the Mount Chapel Country Club, but her application was rejected." A few seconds later, she mumbled, "And hers will be as well."

CHAPTER TWENTY-FOUR

Miss Boo was at a stop sign, lost in her thoughts, when I spoke up. "This is a very nice neighborhood, and Trish and Milton's home is attractive, what we saw of it. A bit gaudy, but attractive."

She shook her head, as if to wake herself up. "Yes, it is," she said. "This whole area is beautiful. The homes are newer than the ones in my neighborhood. These are on the grounds of what used to be Briarwood Plantation, back in the 1800s. There are times I consider selling that giant of a house I live in and buying a one-story more suitable for my needs. Every time I start to get serious about it, something comes along and catches my attention, and I forget about moving. But if I were to move," she said, "I'd certainly consider this area." She looked both ways for traffic. "Or I would have before today," she added then started through the intersection.

"I'm not that familiar with Mount Chapel, but isn't this the neighborhood that's near Briarwood?" I asked. "I thought Milton lived close enough to enter by a back entrance."

"It is. Let me show you just how close." Miss Boo turned onto another street and, after a couple of turns, ended up back where we'd been only a couple of minutes before, in front of Milton and Trish's home. "To go from here to Lorraine's house, you just . . ." Just as we passed the house we'd left only minutes before, the garage door slid upwards.

"Let's play detective," Miss Boo said and pulled over to the curb about half a block farther up the street. She watched in the rearview mirror while I turned to look out the back window as a car backed down the driveway.

"Duck," she said as the object of our surveillance headed our way. We quickly bent our heads, but popped up in time to catch a glimpse of the occupants of the almost new Mercedes as it passed us. "I wonder why she was looking at cars when she already has an almost new one," Miss Boo mused. "Maybe they were shopping for a car for the man who's with her, whoever he is."

"You don't recognize him?" I asked.

"No, but we need to find out," she replied. "That's the man who was at the dealership this morning. He. . . ." She trailed off, leaving her thought unfinished.

"You said she was car shopping for her brother?" I finished her thought.

"Yes, supposedly," she said, "but. . . ."

"But?"

"But I don't know if I believe that or not," she said.

When we wound our way out of the subdivision of luxury homes, Miss Boo took a couple of turns, taking a different path than she had when we'd entered. She pointed to an ornate iron gate set in a brick wall and said, "The back way into Lorraine's property." We'd both stopped calling her LaRue. That was somebody else.

There were vestiges of yellow crime scene tape still attached to the bars of the gate, and there was a sign announcing, 'No admittance: By order of Police Dept.' I wondered if the presence of tape and a sign would deter anyone from entering the property if they wanted to do so. Probably not, I concluded. "Hmm," I responded.

"Yes," she said, agreeing with what I was thinking, whatever it was.

"Close."

"Indeed."

"Handy."

"For?"

I looked at her and raised my eyebrows. "For Milton to go back and forth?"

"Or for murder," she responded.

I had to think about that, and I didn't answer immediately. "Why?" I finally said.

She shook her head and didn't answer. "Wouldn't that stop the income?" I prodded.

"Maybe," she answered. "Maybe not." I spent the rest of the ride puzzling over her answer. How could the LaRue Saint Pierre books continue, even if the real author was still alive, if nobody knew who was really writing the sexy novels? If they needed a female name on the books, Milton still couldn't admit to being LaRue Saint Pierre, not after Lorraine had displayed herself so prominently as being the author. And since the world now knew that the person they knew as LaRue was dead, didn't that end the books, and therefore the income derived from them?

We didn't speak again, and by the time I pulled myself out of my thoughts and into the present time and place, we were back at my office. I took off the glasses, returned them to the glove box, and pinned my nametag back on before opening the door.

"We'll talk," Miss Boo said as I exited her car.

My boss saw me come in. I saw him notice me and take one step toward the front but changed his mind and went back into his private office. I guess he figured it wouldn't gain him anything to come speak to me, that he wouldn't be able to gain any information about where Miss Boo and I had gone nor what we'd learned. He would be right about that. I wasn't about to part with one word of information until I wrote up a story, and what story could I write up right now? None.

I didn't seem appropriate to write that Milton had married a woman he'd met only months earlier while visiting Las Vegas, and I couldn't write that when his sister, Lorraine, died, his bride had changed from a normal, reserved, southern lady into a flashy incarnation of a character from one of LaRue Saint Pierre's books. Nor was it the time to reveal the fact that Milton had ghostwritten the sexy books attributed to his sister. So, what could I write? Nothing. Yet.

I'd been at work about two hours, busily answering the phone, answering questions, and switching calls to various departments, when Miss Boo called. Her message was short. "Come to supper. Don't bring anything. We still have the pie from last time." Then she hung up. It was a good thing I didn't have a date for that evening, but that was a pretty safe assumption. I hadn't been on a date since before the murder drew everyone's attention. My usual date guy was Porter Quinn, and he'd been out of town covering the state legislative session for a while now. He had popped back into town during the hoopla of Lorraine's funeral, and we'd talked, but as soon as things had settled a bit, he'd returned to the capitol.

My other sometimes date person was Asher Donovan, and he was completely tied up in the murder investigation, although I wouldn't be surprised if he turned up at his grandmother's house that evening. He knew Miss Boo and I were involved—he called it snooping—in the secrets Lorraine Coggins had kept hidden from the public. He did not, however, know about our latest discovery, the identity of the person who used the *nom de plu*me LaRue Saint Pierre and had written all the books that Lorraine took credit for.

Sure enough, after work, I'd just pulled into my parking spot and made my way through the hedge separating my residence from Miss Boo's, when Ash drove up and parked behind her home.

"Fancy seeing you here," he quipped.

"You, too," I said.

"I brought my share." He lifted a grease-stained brown paper bag. Even from ten feet away, I caught the aroma of something spicy and delicious. "Tamales," he said, and my mouth immediately started watering.

The tamale lady came by our office as well. She and her mother made the delicious corn-husk-wrapped indulgences and went from business to business peddling them. A dozen of the spicy south-of-the-border treats were reasonably priced but too many for me to buy very often unless I froze some to eat later.

"I'm glad I'm invited for supper," I said. "Those smell so good!"

"I figured I'd bribe Granny Boo." He grinned. "And now I have two people I can persuade to tell me what you two are up to, or I'll eat all the tamales myself."

"That'll probably do it," I answered. Of course, just how much of what we were up to that we'd tell him was the question. That would be up to Miss Boo.

CHAPTER TWENTY-FOUR

Miss Boo was surprised when Ash and I walked in the door together. Larry, smelling the delicious odor that arrived with us, awoke and hopped up from his nap. I didn't blame him. It had me salivating as well.

Miss Boo's eyes widened when she saw her grandson, and she frowned slightly. Asher's presence threw a monkey wrench in her plans to discuss Milton's wife and the possibility of her involvement in her sister-in-law's murder, as well as the identity of the man we saw in the car with her. It seemed to me that there would be plenty to talk about, given Trish's background and our evaluation of what that might entail, but would she want to share that with Ash? I didn't know.

"My goodness, something smells good!" Miss Boo said.

"And it can be yours," Asher said, "if you tell me what you two are up to."

"Up to?" his grandmother asked, trying to look innocent.

"Yes, up to," Ash said. "I saw your car, with you two in it, headed across town. It was during work hours, when Sissy was supposed to be at the *News*. I knew something was up, so I followed you."

"Followed us?" Miss Boo's frown got even stronger. "Asher Donovan! Shame!"

"I thought I might be needed. I never know when I might have to rescue you . . .again."

"Now, that's not at all true. You make it sound like. . . ."

"Like I have to save you from yourself from time to time?"

"I wouldn't put it that way," Miss Boo said. She turned toward the range and stirred something in a big pot simmering on a burner.

Asher edged closer and sniffed. "These tamales would go mighty well with that chili you're cooking."

"They would, wouldn't they?" his grandmother agreed.

"So, what were you two up to over in that area?" He wasn't going to give up his interrogation.

Miss Boo sighed, and looked at me. I shrugged my shoulders. We both knew it was hopeless. We'd end up telling Asher what he wanted to know. Why not tell him now and enjoy a meal of both chili *and* tamales?

"We were making a condolence call."

"A condolence call? Someone else has died?"

"Nobody *else* has died," Miss Boo rejoined. "At least, nobody else I know. We visited Milton's wife. After all, her sister-in-law got murdered, and in Mount Chapel that warrants a condolence call."

"Maybe," Ash said. "If you actually knew her. Knew either one of them. And if it were closer to the time it happened. Like around the time of the funeral instead of days later."

Miss Boo sighed. "Okay, Asher. I give up. Let's serve ourselves, and sit down. I'll tell you all about it while we eat." She went to a nearby cabinet and retrieved three bowls, which she placed beside the stove. From a drawer she withdrew a ladle and dipped it into the bubbling chili.

Asher handed over the sack of tamales and started ladling a bowl of chili, while Miss Boo withdrew the fragrant bundle from the paper bag and put it on a platter before she peeled back the foil, releasing even more of the spicy scent. She placed it in the center of the table, which was already set with plates and silverware, so all we had to do was serve ourselves a bowl of chili and seat ourselves.

"You know," Miss Boo said, "I'm thinking of remodeling. I really don't need a formal dining room. I never use it. We always eat here in the kitchen these days. Or instead of remodeling, I could just build a new home. Something more up-to-date. Something one story. Sooner or later, I'll be too old to manage the flight of stairs. What do you think?"

"Stop trying to change the subject," Asher said. "It won't work."

"Well, I had to try," Miss Boo said, innocently.

"You failed," her grandson said and blew on his spoonful of chili. "Tell all."

"The truth is," Miss Boo started then paused. "We really were making a condolence call."

Ash just looked at her, and he was just shy of glowering.

"Don't look at me like that, Asher. There's more. This morning I was in the Cadillac agency, in the service department, and Tim Nowlin saw me, and . . . .." She related how her favorite car salesman was showing her the latest models when she saw Milton's wife. "She was so changed I almost didn't recognize her."

"Changed how?" Ash asked.

"Before Lorraine's death and at the funeral, she was such a mousy little thing that she blended into the background. But now . . ." she shook her head and started eating. "She's a different person. Different in looks, that is. I assume she's still the same person she's always been on the inside."

Asher scowled. He was transferring a couple of tamales to his plate, so momentarily I wondered if he was frowning because of what he was doing or what Miss Boo had said. "So, define different," he said.

"She looks as if she came directly out of a LaRue Saint Pierre book," his grandmother answered.

"Flashy?" he asked. Miss Boo had just taken a bite of tamale and couldn't answer with a mouth full of food. He looked at me.

"Flashy and then some," I said. "Vegas show girl flashy, which fits, since he met and married her in Vegas."

Ash leaned back and wiped his mouth with his napkin. He looked from me to Miss Boo and back again. He didn't speak, but his look said "tell me more." So I did.

"She had brown hair at the funeral, and it was all pulled back into a bun. Now she's a blonde, what you might call a 'bottle blonde," I said, "and her hair is teased and styled to stand out around her head, like a showgirl."

"And she's busty. Very busty," Miss Boo added.

"Busty?" he questioned.

Miss Boo ignored the question he was asking with that one word, and he looked at me. I put down my fork and used both hands to form shapes in front of my chest.

"Oh. Busty," he said and went back to eating.

"And her clothes," Miss Boo said. She was getting warmed up. "Glitzy." She took another bite of chili.

"Short," I explained. "And tight."

"I get the picture." Ash nodded and ate another spoonful of chili.

The three of us were quiet as we enjoyed our tamales and chili, but after a minute, Miss Boo spoke, "We learned another interesting bit of information." She decided to dole out more information, but slowly, just a little bit at a time.

Asher looked at her and asked, "And what was that?"

"There are more books credited to LaRue Saint Pierre yet to be released."

"So?"

"So, how can that happen, with LaRue supposedly dead?"

Asher didn't answer. He stared off into the distance as he thought about the question. "Lorraine wrote them earlier? Before she was murdered?"

"I imagine that's what the publisher will say, but there's a limit to how many books could reasonably be already written but not released," Miss Boo said. "Two or three at the most, I would think."

"Whoever murdered Lorraine Coggins must not have any financial stake in the money from LaRue Saint Pierre book sales," Ash said. "Or else didn't understand how killing the supposed author would stop the cash flow."

"Or," I started speaking as my brain whirled with ideas, "Somebody else could step into the picture as the author."

"A new LaRue Saint Pierre?" Asher questioned. "Would that work?"

"Not a new LaRue," I said. "LaRue Saint Pierre's sister, a Fifi or a Didi Saint Pierre or someone just as flashy as Lorraine was as LaRue could take over authorship of the books. Except, of course, Milton would continue writing them."

No one spoke for a minute or so. Finally, Asher said, "It might work. Flashy Trish, aka Fifi Saint Pierre, La Rue's supposed sister, would take over authorship of the books. That way, all the profits would go to Milton and Trish instead of being split with another person. And with Milton being the actual author, they'd be getting what they might consider their due."

He sat staring into space as he evaluated the possibility of that scenario working. "A motive for murder," he finally said.

"It sounds like a motive," Miss Boo said, "Except for one thing."

"What's that?" Ash asked.

"I don't think Milton would go along with the scheme. He was really and truly upset by his sister's death. No way in the world would Milton have anything to do with murdering Lorraine, money or no money," she said.

CHAPTER TWENTY-FIVE

Days passed. Miss Boo and I would wave when we passed each other coming or going, but she didn't invite me to supper after work, nor did she show up at the office to carry me off on some secret mission. I didn't see Asher Donovan either.

It was still busy at the *News*. Although the excitement over the murder and subsequent funeral had finally died down, and the throngs of strangers who'd overrun the town had gone home, local merchants had discovered that the ads they'd sponsored more than paid for themselves with new customers, and when they were offered a package deal to continue advertising, many continued.

This produced more hubbub. More conversations. More coming and going. Although I hadn't resumed writing the column about the Mount Chapel library, I was kept busy answering the phone and guiding people to the proper department.

It was the day after we'd shared the chili and tamale dinner that it occurred to me that there had been no mention of the man in Trish's car when we'd told Asher about our visit to Lorraine's sister-in-law. It wasn't that we wanted to keep it a secret—not exactly. We were just so absorbed in the change in Trish that we didn't introduce a new string to pull. And I'd thought of another question that hadn't been answered. Where was Milton while his wife was out looking at new cars with another man? Either there was an innocent explanation for the stranger, or else Trish was cheating on her husband. Which one was it?

I mulled it over. If we'd told Asher about it, as a member of the police force investigating the novelist's murder, he could have found out who the stranger was. Maybe his presence was important, or maybe it wasn't, but it might be helpful to tell Ash about it now. I decided to talk to Miss Boo about it, ask her if we ought to share that information now. Better late than never. But there was a problem with that.

For the first time ever, it was hard to get in touch with my friend and landlady. By the time I'd decided we needed to tell her grandson about the stranger in Trish's car, several days had passed, and when I tried calling her, she didn't answer. This was most unusual, as her phone, like mine, was usually close at hand. I left messages on her voice mail, but she didn't return them.

When I got off work, I slipped through the hedge separating our homes and knocked on her back door, but there was no answer. I even left a note. "Call me" it said. That produced no results either. By this point, I was becoming worried. If she was ill, surely somebody would have contacted me by now. Asher would have told me if she was in the hospital. If she was out of town, she would have let me know herself.

After a couple of days, it dawned on me that I hadn't seen nor, more importantly, *heard* Larry. I was sure that if he were home alone, he would bark at anybody who came to the door. Since there was no sign of him, I had to conclude that Miss Boo had taken him with her wherever she went.

My worry grew until, finally, I was forced to do what I had never done before—call Ash Donovan. I didn't have his private number, so I called the Mount Chapel Police Department's non-emergency number to leave a message.

"Is it an emergency?" the voice on the other end of the line asked.

"Er . . . no. Or maybe. I don't know." Was Miss Boo's disappearance due to an emergency? That's what I was trying to find out.

"Could somebody other than Officer Donovan help you?"

"No." I thought about it for about two seconds and decided I wouldn't get anywhere if I didn't say why I wanted him. "I'm concerned about his grandmother. I haven't seen her in a while, and I wanted to check to see that she is okay."

There was silence, then finally the person on the other end said, "I'll have him call you." A couple of hours later, he did just that.

"Granny Boo is fine," he told me. "I'll have her get in touch with you." He sounded busy and didn't elaborate then hung up. That's okay. I hadn't made the call for any reason other than finding out about my missing landlady, whether she was really missing or just too busy to stay in touch.

Sure enough, when I got off work and went to my car, there was a note stuck under the windshield wiper. "Going to be gone a few days," it said. "Doris and I are going to Memphis to go shopping and to see a display of Egyptian antiques at the Pyramid."

It sounded like an enjoyable trip. Memphis had lots of fun things to do. I'd been to exhibits at the Pyramid, which was an interesting place to visit. There were always a lot of places to go and things to do in Memphis. That should have calmed my mind, but it didn't.

Why didn't she tell me in person? She could have come inside to tell me instead of leaving a note stuck on my car. In addition, the note didn't sound like her, and, more importantly, the handwriting looked off to me. I tried to think of a time I'd seen anything Miss Boo had written, but I couldn't recall one. It kept poking at me. Something was wrong, and it was up to me to find out what.

I was still worrying about it the next day when Asher stopped by my office. He wasn't himself. In other words, he was all business, and he didn't flirt with me. Not one sexy smile. Not one double entendre. Not one finger running over the back of my hand.

"Granny Boo is fine," he said. "She and her friend went to Jackson to go shopping." He didn't even stay long enough for my boss to notice him and come see if some new clue about the murder had surfaced.

I caught him before he went out the door. "Where is Larry?"

He stopped and looked back at me. "Larry?"

"Yes. Larry. The dog."

"I have him," he said. "He's at my place."

After he left, it occurred to me that Miss Boo's note had said she was going to Memphis, but Ash said she was in Jackson. A simple mistake? I didn't think so. It was more like one of them—or maybe both—were lying. But why? And why didn't Miss Boo tell me all this in person? And why not leave Larry with me? If it was because I wasn't home all day, she would have left him at the kennel that boarded dogs. Nothing in his story fit. What was going on?

My anxiety grew by the hour. Only the fact that I was kept busy at work kept me from trying to find out more about what was going on. Finally, two days later, Asher came by the *News* office. He was still not the Ash I knew. He was serious, reserved.

"I need you to come to the station with me," he said.

"Why?" His words scared me. All sorts of terrible things flashed through my head.

He glanced around before he spoke. Nobody was close enough to hear what he was saying, but Gene Hoskins was fast approaching. "I want you to look at a lineup. Maybe identify someone," he said in a low voice.

My boss reached us, and Ash was a bit more outgoing, shaking his hand. "I've come to take Sissy with me again," he said.

"That's fine," Mr. Hoskins said, giving me a serious look, which I interpreted to mean, "Find a story to write," which proved true with his next words. "I'm assuming that these times you come by and take my employee off with you will eventually lead to an exclusive?"

"Yes, they will, Mr. Hoskins. They will," Ash said, still shaking my boss' hand. "Hopefully soon. Very soon."

When we were in Ash's car on the way to the police station, I asked, "So what's going on? Who am I going to identify?"

"It's better I don't tell you anything at this point. It might skew your answers. I'll just say that I want you to look at some people and tell me what you know about them, if anything."

I puzzled over that a minute, then asked, "Tell me this, at least. Is Miss Boo okay?" My heart was pounding so hard I could feel it in my chest. If he told me she was dead, I knew I'd fall apart, and I *never* fell apart about anything.

Asher took his eyes off the road to look at me. He had a surprised look on his face. "Oh sure! She's fine! I didn't know you were worried about her."

I took a deep breath and relaxed. Now that I could release that worry, I could face anything.

"You'll see her later. I don't want you two to talk beforehand. It might influence what you say."

"These last few days, not seeing or talking to her, I've been imagining things, and you being so closemouthed about her I . . ." I shook my head.

"I'm sorry if you've been worried," he said. "If I'd have known that, I would have reassured you. Things have been happening fast, and it's been important that we keep all details quiet at this point. You'll know soon enough."

"It's just that you told me she was in Jackson, then she left me a note that said she was going to Memphis. That left me not knowing who or what to believe. Was she still here, or was she going somewhere? And if she was going somewhere, was it Jackson or Memphis?"

I paused to take a breath and to gather my thoughts. "And that doesn't even touch the question of why. Why was she going someplace else? Was it because she was in danger? What had Miss Boo done that was so dangerous?"

There was a long pause before he spoke again, but finally he said, "I didn't know Granny Boo had been in touch with you."

"Just the note," I said. "So I wouldn't worry. But I still did."

"I guess it wouldn't hurt to tell some of it now. She was in Memphis. We stashed her there because Memphis has an FBI office and agents who could help watch out for her, keep her safe."

"FBI? Keep her safe?"

"Yes. We're playing with the big boys now."

I would have asked more questions, but we arrived at the police station, and Ash pulled into a parking place marked "Official Cars Only." Turning toward me he said, "In hindsight, we probably should have sent you to a safe place as well, but at that point we didn't know you were as involved as you were. Until this morning, we didn't know. . . ." He trailed off, shaking his head. "I should have, though. I should have known." He opened the car door. "It's time to nail this whole thing down," he said before sliding out.

CHAPTER TWENTY-SIX

We entered through the front door, where a woman in uniform was standing behind a counter like the one that kept me separated from whoever walked into the *News* office. She was talking to an irate man before her.

"No sir. That's not against the law. You're going to have to live with it."

My first thought was that I was lucky that I didn't have angry people I had to deal with in person. Generally, people who were mad at the *News* yelled at us over the phone instead of coming into the office. Then I wondered what this particular complaint was all about, and if it would be fodder for a story in the paper. We passed on through the area before I heard anything more, but it stirred my imagination, and I wondered if my boss would be interested in a column in the weekly *Mount Chapel News* that related some of the interesting complaints and reports that were made to the local police department. I'd save that idea for later, after this murder investigation was over. I had entirely too many things to think about already without a new column taking up space in my brain.

"Come this way," Asher prompted as he urged me through a door into a large room filled with desks and busy people. Officers, both in uniform and in regular clothing, were typing on computers or talking on phones. They ignored us as we passed through and entered a hall leading further into the interior of the building.

"Just down here," Ash said as we walked down the quiet hallway. Finally, he opened a door and, with a spread of his arm, ushered me into a small room. I had seen places like this on TV shows. There was a large window which looked into the next room, empty of people or furniture. The numbers one through five were painted on the wall, and I'd watched enough episodes of *Law and Order* to know that shortly there would be people to stand before the numbers on the wall, and, most likely, I'd be asked questions about them. If I'd ever seen them before, for instance, or similar questions.

Asher verified that when he said, "In a few minutes, I'm going to ask you to tell me if you've seen some people before, and if so, where. Think you can do that?"

"Just like on TV, huh?"

"Yeah. Just like on TV," he responded.

"Sure," I answered.

"They won't be able to see you," he assured me. "You will be able to say whatever you want, and they won't hear you."

I noticed the thick glass in the window, and also that the room we were in was dimly lit, while the lights were very bright on the other side.

"Okay. That's good."

"I'll go tell them we're ready," Ash said, his hand on the doorknob. "You can have a seat if you want."

I looked around and saw several chairs, nice-looking office chairs, all facing the window. Evidently the Mount Chapel police wanted folks to be comfortable as they identified suspects.

"Okay?" Ash asked, frowning. Did he think I might become overwhelmed or scared or something? Would he not open the door to leave until he was sure I would be okay? I was touched by what I interpreted as concern.

"Sure," I said and smiled. "I can handle that. No worries."

He gave a little smile back and left. I wandered around the small room, not that there was much space for wandering or much to see. Basically just the chairs and a table against the back wall. It could be pulled to the center of the small room and encircled with the chairs. That way the space could be used for other purposes as well. I wouldn't think Mount Chapel would have lineups very often. Asher hadn't given me so much as a clue as to what was happening. Maybe he thought that since the incident his grandmother and I had been through down on the coast, I would be familiar with lineups and such, but I wasn't. Finally, I took a seat facing the window, ready to look at whoever I was tasked to identify.

There was nothing much to see or puzzle about, so time passed slowly. It seemed like a long time, but it was probably less than ten minutes before the door opened and Ash was back. "Ready?" he asked.

"Ready," I responded and watched as men started filing into the brightly lit room on the other side of the glass.

"Take a good look," Ash said, "You can take your time to study them. If you've seen one of them before, tell me where and under what circumstances. They can't see into this room," he repeated what he had told me earlier, "so don't worry about them knowing who's identifying them." He paused as numbers one and two took places before the numbers on the wall. "You can take all the time you need," he repeated. I thought he sounded a bit nervous. Surely they didn't have to do this—have lineups—very often in Mount Chapel. Especially since it had to do with the murder of such a famous person as LaRue Saint Pierre. Or even Lorraine Coggins.

"This shouldn't take long," I said as number three took his place. "I know them all."

He gave me a look that said, "you're kidding" but he didn't say a word. He opened his mouth as if he was going to speak, but he thought better of it. Instead, he went to a small metal box beside the window, obviously a speaker into the next room, and pushed a button. "Number one, step forward," he said, and a tall guy with longish hair pulled back into a ponytail moved closer to the window.

"That's Bill Norwood," I said. "He's a waiter at the Italian Villa over in Oak Springs. Porter takes me to dinner there sometimes when we go to the movies or some other event. He's always friendly and gets our order right. I don't know anything else about him, and I've never seen him any other place but where he works."

Asher was frowning, and I hoped it was because he caught that I dated Porter Quinn on occasion, and that he took me out for dinner and entertainment, unlike Asher, who only flirted and stole kisses when he could get by with it but never took me out, like on a date.

"Oh, I do know something else about him," I said. "He's saving up money to take classes on something . . . criminal justice, I think. He says he wants to have a career, not just a job. Admirable, don't you think? I don't know why he's in this lineup, but I hope it's nothing serious."

Asher didn't respond to me but pushed the button on the intercom or whatever it was and said, "Number one, step back." He waited a few seconds as Bill returned to his original spot then said, "Number two, step forward."

The next man was taller by an inch or so. He was the most muscular man in the line. His hair was brown with a reddish tint to it. I had recognized him the minute he walked into the room. "That's Russ," I said. "I don't know his last name. He delivers packages. He's in and out of the *News* office about every week, and sometimes more often, bringing something to someone. I see him all over town. He almost always has a box in his hands and is in a hurry. I think he has a tight time schedule." I stopped talking and sent another smile toward Asher. He didn't return it.

"Number two, step back; Number three, step forward," he said into the speaker. *So there for doubting what I said,* I almost said out loud.

The next man was the shortest man in the line, as well as not as *big*. He was what people often referred to as wiry. His clothing, jeans and an old Guns and Roses tee shirt, looked like they had come from a donation bin somewhere. I grinned and looked at Asher. "Shame on you," I said. "Trying to trick me."

"Trick you?" he said and his eyebrows raised even higher.

"Absolutely," I said. "That's Newby Forrester. He's an undercover cop. Everybody in town knows it. I know it and you know it and now you know that I know."

"How. . .?" He stared at me. "Why do you say that?" Asher asked. "If he is, as you say, undercover, then nobody knows he's a cop."

"Asher, come on! *Everybody* in Mount Chapel knows Newby's a cop. How does he ever catch anyone doing anything illegal when everyone knows who he is?"

Ash just grinned, the first honest grin he'd given me that day, and said, "People in other towns don't know he's a cop."

"So you recruit people to fill spots in lineups?"

"Yeah, we have a list."

"A list of innocent men?"

"People who volunteer to help us out," he explained. "And you are absolutely not to tell anyone that bit of information, including writing about it." His expression was firm as he looked at me. "Understand?"

"I've got it," I agreed. "I'll never tell. What happens if the person in my spot, the person doing the identifying, picks out one of the good guys as being the person who did whatever?"

"Then we know that they don't have very good observation skills, and we might not be able to use their version of what happened," Ash said and paused. "And you absolutely cannot put that in the newspaper either," he cautioned me.

He pushed the button again. "Number three, step back. Number four, step forward."

There were five spots for people in the lineup, but only four of them were filled. When we first started, I had spouted off about knowing the people in the brightly lit room, but I'd only glanced at them as they filed in, and, when I recognized the first few, I stopped looking. This one, number four, took my breath away.

It was the man who'd been in the car with Trish the day Miss Boo and I had pulled to the side of the street a few doors away from Milton and Trish's house. He was darker complexioned than the others, like he had a deep sun tan, or else he was from a heritage of dark-skinned people. Italian, maybe, or Spanish. Brown hair was smoothly combed into what I think they called a pompadour back in the day. Where the expressions on the faces of the first three men were neutral, his was evil, like the bad man in a movie just before he pulled the trigger to murder somebody. His eyes seemed to drill holes in the glass right at me, and even though common sense told me that he couldn't see through the window that separated us, I still shivered. It was as if he were threatening whoever was on the other side of the glass. *I identify me, and it'll be the last thing you ever do.*

When I didn't speak, Asher finally asked, "What about the last man? Have you ever seen him before?" And I managed to nod my head.

"You have?" he sounded surprised. "Where? And when?"

I had to clear my throat before I could speak, trying to get rid of the fear that irrationally built up in me, even though common sense told me that he didn't know who was on the other side of the glass. "He was in the car with Milton's wife the day Miss Boo and I went to visit her. We saw them leaving."

Ash just stared at me for a few seconds then finally asked, "Were you with her at the car agency that morning?"

"No, but she told me about it," I said, shaking my head. "She said she saw him there with Trish Coggins. They were car shopping. That's what made her decide we needed to pay a condolence call to Milton and Trish. Maybe we could find out who he was, and what was going on."

"And this guy," Ash nodded his head toward the lineup in the next room, "was there at their house?"

"Not exactly," I explained. "Just Trish was there. Milton wasn't—Trish said that he'd gone to New York to meet with the editor of the LaRue Saint Pierre books. We saw this man in Trish's car with her after we left, so thinking back on it, he must have been there, in the house, when we were there but stayed out of sight."

Asher looked puzzled, so I explained, "We'd circled around so Miss Boo could show me the way Milton would go from his house to Lorraine's, when we saw them pull out of the garage at Milton and Trish's house."

"And they saw you?"

"Maybe. We ducked down, but I guess they could have seen us."

Asher swore under his breath. He just stood there a bit then pushed the speaker button one more time and said, "You can step back, number four," and released it.

"I'll be back," he said, "Just relax," and he left the room.

A couple of minutes later, the men in the lineup filed out, and the lights in the next room lowered to a normal level instead of the bright glare of earlier. I sat there, trying unsuccessfully to think of happier things, wishing that the feeling of dread that had come upon me would go away.

CHAPTER TWENTY-SEVEN

It seemed like forever before Asher came back, but it probably was only ten minutes or so. Time flies when you're busy and happy but drags when you're sitting in a dark room worrying about a man in a lineup. Worrying about who he might be or what he might be guilty of doing. Was it possible that he had anything to do with Lorraine's death?

I was thinking about that when Ash came back. "You were a big help," he said. "I'd like to move you to a more comfortable room. We might have more questions. Think Gene would mind if you stay longer?"

"I think Gene Hoskins would let me stay here at the police department full time if it meant I'd get a story out of it," I said. "Especially if the story has to do with the death of a famous novelist with roots in Mount Chapel."

"Oh, there'll be a story, but not right now. Not today," he said. "But soon."

"Soon?"

"Don't push it," he warned. He held the door into the hall wide open. "Come this way."

I followed him down the hall and around a corner. At the junction, there were large panels to separate the two different areas. They were standing open but could be easily closed and locked securely. The entrance we'd entered earlier was to the police department and all its functions, while this hall and the rooms on either side were the premises for other city-related functions.

We stopped before a room labeled, "Conference Room A." The first thing I saw when Asher opened the door was Miss Boo. She jumped up from where she was seated and hurriedly threw her arms around me.

"Oh, I'm so glad you're safe!" she said. "I've been so worried. Nobody would tell me a thing." When she released her hold, she held me at arm's length to examine me, as if she was looking me over to see if I was okay.

"I've been worried about you too," I replied. "And the same thing goes. Your note said you were going to Memphis, but Asher told me you were in Jackson. That scared me, saying different cities like that. It was proof there was a reason to lie about where you were."

"I got fussed at for leaving that note," she said, releasing her hold on me. "I wasn't supposed to tell *anybody* where I was going to be, or be in touch with anyone once I was there."

"If anyone had caught that you were there when Granny Boo saw that man, you would've been in protective custody along with her," Ash said. "In Memphis. But . . ." he said to Miss Boo, "telling where you were could have gotten you killed. We're dealing with dangerous people here."

"I'm glad I was in Memphis instead of Jackson," Miss Boo said. "There's so much to see and do in Memphis. And the nicest young man went along with me to keep me safe."

Ash shook his head. "I'm sure the FBI office in Memphis will never be the same after babysitting Granny Boo." He moved toward the door. "You two hang tight. Don't leave this room." He waved his hand toward a door on the back wall. "There's a rest room through there. I'll be back in a few."

"I hope that when you come back, you can tell us what's going on," Miss Boo called out as he left.

"Maybe," Ash answered. "If I can." He showed just a bit of his crooked smile then left the room.

"Let's sit," Miss Boo said, and we settled into two of the chairs that surrounded the table in the middle of the room, which was quite a bit larger than the one I'd been sequestered in previously. This was obviously a meeting space for people who were higher on the totem pole than those who were looking at a lineup of supposed criminals on the other side of a window. I doubted that a criminal ever set foot in this space. The centerpiece was a highly polished table with room for a dozen or so people. Leather upholstered chairs surrounded it. Mount Chapel leaders would be in stylish comfort as they met to discuss and solve problems.

"The FBI was very accommodating," she said. "When they realized they weren't going to keep me in my hotel room, as nice as it was, they sent the most pleasant young man with me everywhere I went, and Memphis has a lot of places to go." She settled herself into a chair before continuing. "And when we went back to the hotel," she said, "a young woman took over. She even spent the night watching over me, to keep me safe in case bad guys figured out where I was. I had a suite, you know, and she slept on the sofa—if she slept at all, that is."

She skipped quickly over the idea that she might be in danger from anybody, moving to more pleasant subjects. "I insisted on choosing where I was to stay. I told them I'd even pay for it myself, but I was not going to be staying at some out-of-the-way hotel or motel. I could be just as safe in a nice place, maybe safer since the bad guys might not think of looking for me there. I chose the Peabody, which is known for its luxury. Have you ever visited the Peabody?"

"No, ma'am. But I've heard about it. Everybody has heard about the Peabody ducks. That must be something to see."

"Yes, it is," she agreed. "I always enjoy seeing those ducks parading out of the elevator and crossing the lobby to the duck pond. I wonder how they trained them to do that," she mused. "When all this is over and we can go where we want and not be frightened of whoever it is we're frightened of, you and I are going to have to visit Memphis and stay at the Peabody."

"I think the Peabody would be out of my budget," I said. "I hear that it's expensive. *Very* expensive."

"Don't worry about that," Miss Boo said, giving a dismissive swipe in the air. "I'll pay for it. It probably was out of the FBI's budget, but I insisted that if I was going to be held someplace incognito, then it had to be someplace like the Peabody or better, even if I had to pay for it myself."

"I don't even know if I get any vacation time," I said. "It's never been brought up."

"We'll just have to come up with a story for you to write, so going to Memphis would be on the clock, so to speak."

"Maybe that would work," I said. "I imagine there's a lot of things to write about in Memphis, but I don't know about a job-related story. I'd just have to think of how to tie it into Mount Chapel. Maybe a series of articles about what to see and do when you visit Memphis."

"There's Graceland, of course," Miss Boo said. "Lots of folks are besotted with anything Elvis related. Personally, I liked his singing, but I don't need to see the house he bought for his mama. There's plenty of other places that are more interesting, at least to me. There was an arts and crafts fair happening at the convention center and a fine arts display at the Pyramid. And there's the zoo. I always like to visit a zoo, and Memphis has a good one. Of course, there's always shopping."

We spent some time discussing the pros and cons of Memphis, so—like the saying—time sped by and before we knew it, Asher was back. He was accompanied by two men I didn't know.

"Ladies, these two gentlemen are with the FBI. They'd like to talk with you and ask some questions."

"Mrs. Bryce, Miss Townley, my name is Douglas Baker. This," he said, nodding his head toward the other man, "is Bryan Foster. How would you like to work with the FBI?"

CHAPTER TWENTY-EIGHT

Three days later, when I arrived at the *News*, Gene Hoskins met me right up front. "Cecelia," he said in a loud voice, "You might as well not sit down. I'm tired of you going off with Boo Bryce for lunch and staying gone for hours. Everybody else has to do the jobs I've been paying *you* to do. I hired you in the first place just as a favor to my friend of many years, but it's just not working. You're fired."

I tried to protest. "But . . ." I started, but he turned and walked away. Everybody was staring at me as I stood there, stricken. I finally turned and left. Even though it was all pretend, it still got to me, and it wasn't hard to act like I'd really been fired.

Before I even pulled out of the parking lot, I called Miss Boo. "It's done," I said. "He was kind of dramatic about it—almost over the top."

"That's Gene for you," she responded. "How about getting us a couple of breakfast sandwiches," she said. "Make mine ham, egg, and cheese. I have orange juice."

When I walked into her kitchen, Larry was in the yard, but the scent of good things to eat tempted him to follow me back into the house. The smell of coffee filled the air and glasses of juice were already on the table.

"I've been thinking about our next step," she said as she peeled the wrapper from her English muffin. "I'm going to call the country club and reserve a table for lunch." She took a bite. A minute later, she continued explaining her plan. "Then I'll call Trish and invite her to eat with us."

She frowned as she ate and thought. "Maybe I won't mention you. You'll be there, but if she thinks it will just be the two of us, that I'm specifically inviting her . . ." she trailed off and took another bite.

"It'll make her feel special," I said. "If she thinks it'll just be the two of you."

"Exactly," she agreed.

When I finished my sandwich and wadded the paper wrapper, I got up and threw it into the garbage. "You're going to call Asher?" I asked as I walked back toward the table. "To tell him we're ready?"

"Yes. He'll take care of the rest."

I went back to my apartment, where I tried to decide what clothing to wear in order to look dowdy. It went against my nature to actually try to *not* look good, but I finally came up with an outfit that looked like it was designed by somebody who didn't know anything about matching their clothes and cared even less. Later, when Miss Boo and I left, I retrieved the eyeglasses from her glove box, slid them on, and gave my hair a final tousle. Settling my psyche into being drab Sissy Townley, assistant and companion to the richest person in Mount Chapel, I tried to quell my nervous thoughts.

Cecelia Townley, reporter, was gone. She'd been fired, and Sissy Townley was a completely different person, a nobody. Those folks who thought they were the same person were wrong. Can't you tell by looking?

When we reached the country club, we saw the familiar Mercedes, the one that sped by us when we were parked down the street from Milton and Trish's house. When Miss Boo pulled into the empty spot next to it, the driver's door opened, and Trish stepped out.

"I'm so glad you could make it, Trish," Miss Boo said. "I had meant to be back in touch with you before now, but business called me out of town. I've been attending some very boring board of directors' meetings, and I've only been back a few days."

Trish Coggins looked flustered. "I'm glad you suggested lunch today," she said. "I didn't hear from you since the day you dropped by my house, and I thought I must have said something inappropriate."

"Not at all, Trish. Not at all. As I said on the phone earlier, I was suddenly called out of town to deal with business matters. But I'm back now!" She looped her arm through Trish's and drew her along with us, urging her toward the front door of the exclusive club that served the upper-class citizens of Mount Chapel. "Come along, Sissy," she urged then turned her attention back to our mark. "They have an excellent chef. Have you eaten here before?" She ignored the fact that Trish didn't answer.

When we entered the majestic dining room, the maître d' greeted us. "So glad to see you today, Mrs. Bryce. Your table is this way." He led us to a round table overlooking the golf course and pulled out a chair for Miss Boo then hurried to seat Trish. I was left to fend for myself.

Three menus were laying at an empty spot, and he opened them one by one and placed them before us. "William will be your server today." He gave a slight bow and left.

I was studying the menu when William arrived. When I looked up, I was startled to see the man I'd recently seen in the police lineup and before that at the Italian Villa. He was pouring water into the goblets before us. When he saw that I recognized him, he gave the smallest of winks, followed by the slightest shake of his head, and a frown.

"Good afternoon, ladies. My name is William. I'll be your waiter today. May I get you something else to drink? Sweet or unsweet tea perhaps? Or wine? We have an especially fine selection of both red and white, locally produced." He ended up looking to Miss Boo, recognizing her as the leader of the group.

"No, thank you, William. Water is fine for me," Miss Boo said. "Ladies?" she asked as she looked back and forth between Trish and myself.

I murmured my refusal and took a sip of water to acknowledge my choice. Trish shook her head as well. I would have thought that she would have been at ease in this situation, since she must have ordered food and drink often in Las Vegas, but she acted edgy.

Miss Boo led the conversation as we ate, and nothing controversial was brought up, nor did she take the subject to anything other than the most casual topics. The meal had almost ended when Trish, acting more nervous by the minute, announced, "I have some news to share with you. Milton wanted me to keep it quiet for a bit longer, but you have been so friendly, Mrs. Bryce, that I wanted you to be the first to know."

Maybe Trish was more perceptive than I thought. She'd picked up on the subtle reprimand at our last meeting when she'd called the grand dame of Mount Chapel "Miss Boo", a name that only close friends and lifelong acquaintances used.

"My husband, Milton, has recently returned from New York, where he met with the publisher of his sister's books. I believe I mentioned that she had a couple of manuscripts ready to be published and after that, nothing.

"Her fans are begging for more, so . . ." She came to a stop, looking at Miss Boo for long seconds before completing her thought. "I'm going to take up where she left off. Under another pen name, of course." She took a sip of water before continuing, "I won't be using the name LaRue Saint Pierre. That was Lorraine. I'll be writing under a pen name as well, and the publicity will say that I am LaRue's younger sister." She took another sip of water, probably to wet a dry mouth. "Which I am, in a way. I'm her sister-in-law, which is kind of a sister."

Miss Boo and I both were speechless. Speechless and motionless. What do you say to such an announcement? After holding our thoughts a couple of seconds, attempting to form a reasonable response, I murmured a muddled answer, and Miss Boo finally spoke.

"And who will be writing the books?"

"I will," Trish replied.

"I see. You have experience writing novels, then?" Miss Boo queried.

"Not commercially, but I took writing in college," Trish answered. "I made good grades—A or A plus—and my teachers thought I should pursue a career as an author."

Miss Boo shot a glance at me, and when I saw her eyes open wide and her lips press tightly together, I knew she was holding in laughter and inappropriate comments. We both knew who would continue writing the popular novels. Milton. What we knew so far about Trish did not suggest that she could write so much as a grocery list, much less a whole book. As hard as it must have been for Lorraine to have passed as the author of numerous novels, it would be even harder for Trish.

I could see how the new arrangement would benefit both Milton and his wife. The quality of the writing wouldn't change, since he would continue to ghostwrite, just as he had before Lorraine's death. The money advances and the royalties would all go to the couple, instead of being split between brother and sister. Although that made a motive for one of them to be the killer even stronger, I still couldn't imagine Milton killing Lorraine. Would Trish be motivated enough to kill her husband's sister without his approval?

"I'm looking forward to reading some of your work, Trish," Miss Boo finally pulled herself together enough to say. "Have you chosen a pen name to use on your work?"

"I'm not set on one yet," Trish said. "There are several I'm thinking of. Trixie or Bunny, maybe. My parents used to call me Bunny, and some old friends still use that name."

"Will you still use the same last name? Saint Pierre?" Miss Boo enquired.

"Yes. The publisher thinks I should because of name recognition," Trish answered.

I'm glad I wasn't expected to comment or ask a question. I couldn't have come up with anything appropriate under the circumstances, and if I had to speak I might have broken into giggles at the thought of Trish as an author.

Before long, the meal was over, and as we rose to leave. Miss Boo said, "This has been delightful. We'll have to do it again sometime." When the three of us reached the other side of the room, I was trailing behind my companions. When I looked back at the table where we'd spent the last hour, I saw William doing exactly what he was there to do. Taking a napkin in hand, he carefully picked up Trish's water glass, and, after pouring the last few drops into another goblet, he carefully wrapped it. Before the last turn of fabric, he took the fork she had used, placed it next to the goblet in his hand and enveloped it as well. Ignoring the rest of the table, he nodded to the maître d' and left the room, carrying the bundle he'd been sent to obtain.

The three of us walked together to our cars. Trish seemed much more at ease. She'd passed whatever test she'd set for herself, likely that of what she considered believability, and she was convinced that she'd been accepted into the upper echelons of Mount Chapel society by way of Miss Boo, even if she did have to address her as Mrs. Bryce.

If she'd heard our conversation on the way back to Miss Boo's house, she would have been disabused of that idea. Although there were few words spoken on that short trip, they weren't words favorable to Trish Coggins. Or Bunny Saint Pierre. Or whoever she would end up being.

When Miss Boo pulled into her usual parking spot behind her house, she said, "I wonder how long it will take?"

I knew just what she was referring to. "Can they check the prints here in Mount Chapel, or will they have to send them to Las Vegas?"

"I don't know," she answered. "We need to ask Asher. I'll call and invite him to supper."

"I think I'll just go to my place for now," I said as I got out of her car. "I'm going to write all this up while it's fresh in my mind so as to be ready when the time comes."

"That's a good idea," she replied. "You'll be ready for publication when you go back to work."

CHAPTER TWENTY-NINE

That's exactly what I did—write a column for the newspaper I'd been fired from earlier in the day. I saved it for when it was needed, for when my public firing was rescinded, and I returned to work at the *News* to tell the rest of the story.

Then I proceeded to return my appearance to normal, that is to say, I erased the dull and unfashionable Sissy and replaced her with the chic Sissy. No way did I want to appear frumpy when Asher Donovan came to dinner.

When I was finally satisfied with what I saw in the mirror—skinny jeans and a tee, hair artfully curled, glossy lips, eyelashes darkened—I started toward the door. At the last minute, I went back to my dressing table and added one more touch, a small silver heart on a chain that was just the right length to catch Ash's attention.

When I opened the door into Miss Boo's kitchen, the aroma that reached my nose had me rethinking my promise to myself—the one about not eating so much when Miss Boo invites me for supper. So far I'd managed to keep from gaining weight, but that would change if I ate with Miss Boo often.

"If you're as full as I am after that lunch we had," she said, "you probably don't want much. The last time I cooked pot roast, I froze half of it. Asher loves my pot roast. Maybe this will butter him up."

I started setting the table for three. "It smells wonderful," I said. "But you're right. I don't want much."

"Did you get your column written?"

"I did," I replied. "Ready for when we can tell the story."

"Asher acted oddly when I called him," she said. "I'd like to know what's going on."

"Oddly?"

"I called and asked him to dinner, and he said, 'I'll get back to you on that,' and hung up."

"He must be busy." I retrieved plates from the cabinet and started placing them before the places that had become our usual seating spots.

"Or couldn't talk in front of somebody."

"That too."

"He called back about an hour later and said, 'I think I'll be able to make it,' then hung up."

"I wonder if those two FBI agents were there," I mused.

"I think they're running the whole thing, whatever it is," Miss Boo said.

"I got that impression too," I said.

"So Asher might not be able to tell us as much about what's going on as he usually does."

"You're right," I agreed. "He sure doesn't want to get on the bad side of the feds."

It was another half-hour before Ash arrived, and, when he did, he acted like he weighed every word before speaking. "There are things I can't talk about," he explained.

"Will you be able to someday?" I asked.

"Maybe," was his response. I'd have to be satisfied with that. "Probably."

"We were surprised to see the young man who was in the lineup waiting tables at the country club today," Miss Boo said. "So obviously he was planted there."

"Yes, he was. We often call on people to fill out a group for identity purposes," Ash said. "Men or women who fit the general description of the person we suspect of wrongdoing."

"I think I knew that already," she replied. "But I was talking about working at the country club. He was planted there, wasn't he?"

Asher placed his fork on his plate and leaned on his elbows as he looked from his grandmother to me and back again. "He could have been," he said. "But waiting tables is the way he makes his living while attending college."

"He's studying criminal justice, right?" I asked.

"Right," he confirmed. "He wants to work for the FBI when he gets his degree."

"So, he works for the local police when you need him," I commented.

"Sort of. He doesn't exactly 'work' for us, usually when we need someone of his description to be in a lineup."

"And to collect fingerprints," Miss Boo said.

He stared at her. "No comment," he said and went back to eating. "This is good, Granny Boo, You ought to fix it more often," he said, trying to steer the conversation in a different direction.

"I saw him," I said. "I saw him take the glass and the fork. Before that, I might have thought that he worked as a waiter at more than one place, but I looked back. . . ."

"I'll have to caution him," Ash said, shaking his head. "If we ever have need for him to do something similar again. He should wait longer, until whoever we're watching is long gone, or take the items to the back, as if he was just bussing the table."

"We learned something new at the luncheon," Miss Boo said.

"What's that?" Asher inquired.

"Milton is working out something with Lorraine's publisher, and Trish is going to write the novels from now on. Not as LaRue Saint Pierre, of course. She'll have her own pen name. She's thinking about using Bunny Saint Pierre as her *nom de plume*."

Ash looked at his grandmother in surprise. "I didn't know she could write," he said.

"She probably can't," Miss Boo said. "Although she tried to convince us otherwise."

We finished the meal with a dish of ice cream. When I yawned, I said, "I think I need to go home and go to bed. This has been a busy day."

"I need to talk to you, both of you, about something," Ash said. "We're dealing with some very bad people here. Sissy, you don't have any kind of security system at your apartment, right?"

"That's right."

"I think you ought to move over here to Granny's house until we wrap this thing up. You have an empty bedroom, don't you?" he asked his grandmother.

"Of course. More than one," she replied. "That's an excellent idea, Asher."

"You really think I might be in danger?"

"I don't want to think that, but it's better to be cautious."

"That's an excellent idea, Asher. Sissy, why don't you go pack a bag now, while he can go with you."

I thought about it, but not for long. I'm a big scaredy-cat. "Okay. I guess that would be a good idea."

"And Granny Boo, I'll bet you don't turn on the burglar alarm half the time, do you?"

She looked guilty and answered. "Well. . . ."

"Do it religiously, starting right now. Turn it on when we leave. You can come let us back in. I'll go with Sissy and stay with her while she packs a suitcase." He looked stern as he gave the orders. "And keep it on all the time."

"Yes, Asher. I will."

"And let Larry out by himself—don't go out with him. Watch before you open the door to let him out or back in."

Miss Boo nodded. "I understand."

When we climbed the stairs to my home over the garage, he kept his hand on the gun on his belt, usually hidden by his jacket. As I packed my bag, he paced around checking the locks on the windows, and when I had everything I thought I needed and headed toward the door, he stopped me with a hand on my arm. "Sissy. . . ."

"Yes?"

The kiss caught me by surprise. Sweet and soft and above all, caring.

"Be careful. These are very bad people we're dealing with," he said before he released me.

When we crossed into Miss Boo's backyard, Larry was there, sniffing the bushes and lifting his leg at various spots. "He's a good watch dog," Ash said. "He'll let you know if anybody is sneaking around." He rapped lightly on the back door. Miss Boo had lowered the shade over the window and pulled it aside to be sure it was us before she unlocked and opened the door.

"Asher, you do have a key to my house, don't you?" she asked her grandson.

"I do. One for this door and one for the front. They're on my keyring."

"I thought you did," she said. "Good!"

He put his arm around her shoulders and pulled her into a hug. "Please be careful," he said. "Don't let a stranger in."

Miss Boo almost sounded teary when she answered. "Now you know what I feel like when you're out there protecting the town and wearing disguises to catch bad guys. You be careful too, Asher."

CHAPTER THIRTY

Miss Boo's guest room was pure luxury to somebody whose bedroom wasn't, to put it kindly, not terribly neat nor well decorated. It was more like the posh suite where we stayed down on the coast when we first met. The next morning when I got up, dressed, and went downstairs, I told her so.

"The downstairs is for living," she said, "but the upstairs doesn't get as much wear and tear. The problem is that, as I grow older, managing the steps becomes more of a problem, and that isn't going to get any better. I really am thinking about looking for a one-story home."

"I can see where it could be a problem, going up and down," I agreed. "It would be handier if everything was all on one level."

"I could turn the library into a bedroom, but I really don't want to do that."

"That would be an answer," I agreed, "but. . . ."

"But upstairs I have my own private bathroom attached." She stared off into space. "And there's no tub or shower on the first floor, and I'd have to give up space somewhere to add one." She sighed and took a sip of coffee.

Just then her phone, which was on the table by her elbow, rang. She checked to see who was calling before she answered.

"Good morning, Asher! How are you this morning?"

I couldn't hear his answer, only her reply. "I'm fine, just fine. Let me switch this so Sissy can hear you, too." She took it away from her ear and laid it on the table. "Now we both can hear you. Is there any progress on the case?"

"Not that I can tell you about," he replied.

"Then we still have to be watching over our shoulder for bad men."

"Definitely. You two stay inside. Don't go anywhere until I tell you it's okay."

"Asher, you know that Sissy and I get along just fine. We enjoy each other's company. But we enjoy the company of others as well," she answered.

"You wouldn't enjoy the company of the people I'm talking about."

"How about the company of safe people?"

"I'd have to think about it." He didn't sound favorable to the idea. "Who are you considering?"

"Doris Benton. She's my best friend, and we see each other several times a week. You know she's safe."

"Mrs. Benton is okay, but you would have to check and see that she's alone."

"Asher, you know I have those fancy camera doorbells at both doors. Just because I seldom use them doesn't mean—"

"Seldom? It's more like never. I wondered why you spent all that money for them when you never check to see who's at the door. You just open it."

"Grace Higgins' grandson was selling them, and he talked me into buying them."

"Well, now you get to use them. But you have to be sure Mrs. Benton is alone, that there's nobody out of sight that could push their way in with her."

"Maybe have a password?"

"Password. Yeah, that would work." Ash sounded impatient. "I've got things to do, catch the bad guys and all that. You be careful and stay safe. I'll check with you later. Bye,"

"Bye, Sweetie. You stay safe, too."

When Miss Boo hung up, I said, "I'm going upstairs and brush my teeth. I'll be back shortly." I put my dishes in the dishwasher before climbing the stairs to my temporary quarters. I wanted to add a bit of makeup and check my hair as well, just in case Asher decided to come by.

When I returned to the kitchen, Miss Boo was on her phone with Doris Benton. "That would be great. Just get anything that looks good. I'll fix tea to drink." There was a pause. "Okay. Remember, everything is copacetic. Bye."

"Everything is copacetic?" I asked when she hung up.

"That's our secret password. Back when we were teenagers, there was a disc jockey on the radio that used that phrase on his program, and we started using it as well, until it finally went out of style. It means everything is okay."

"That sounds about right," I said. "For sure nobody else will know it."

"Yes, and nobody will use it accidentally."

Miss Boo and I went around to every window on the first floor, closing blinds and pulling down shades. That didn't take very long, but we took our time, and as we went from room to room, Miss Boo told me stories about how she had obtained some of the items in her home.

"My son, Super, painted these pictures when he was in the first grade," she said as we closed blinds and pulled the drapes together in the library. "He was so proud of them that I had them framed."

"I assume that Super is just a nickname. How did he get it?" I asked.

She chuckled. "It's funny now, but it wasn't funny when the incident that earned him that name happened.

"We lived in the country back then, in the house where he lives now. He was fascinated with Superman—had everything Superman he could find. He loved to play as if he were Superman. One day, he put a red towel around his shoulders and pinned it together in front. Then he climbed up into the hayloft, and, convinced that as Superman he could fly, he jumped off."

"Oh, no! Was he hurt badly?"

"He was lucky. He came away with only a broken arm. It could have been so much worse." She shook her head. "From there on, everybody called him Super. Most people these days think it's his real name."

As we went from room to room, Miss Boo told me many things about her life and times, and before long the doorbell chimed once, the signal for the back entrance.

"That's probably Doris," she said, and we headed to the kitchen. Pushing the button on the speaker beside the door, she said, "What's the password? And Mrs. Benton replied, "Everything is copacetic," and Miss Boo unlocked three different locks to admit her friend.

"This is like being in a spy movie," Doris Benton said.

"You say that now," Miss Boo responded as she turned all three locks back to the safety settings. "But it won't be funny when we get tired of this."

"It won't last forever," Mrs. Benton replied. "I brought Chinese." She put the aromatic bag of food on the kitchen counter.

"That sounds perfect," Miss Boo said. "I haven't had Chinese in months. It's a bit early for lunch, but Chinese is easy to warm up."

"How are you doing, Sissy? Boo has been telling me about what's going on. I'm sworn to secrecy."

"It's sort of scary," I answered. "We're taking our orders from the FBI these days. I don't know exactly what that means, expect that Lorraine's murder reaches out farther than just Mount Chapel."

"My goodness!" She turned to Miss Boo and asked, "Do you have any idea how long you will have to stay out of sight?"

"I don't have a clue," she answered. "But if it's going to be a long time, maybe we ought to think about waiting it out someplace else, like Hawaii or Ireland."

"Really?" I asked.

"Well, I've always wanted to go to those places, and if I'm going to have to stay inside my house, then maybe it would be time to take a vacation until the danger is over."

I didn't say anything, but I was thinking that I couldn't afford a trip to anywhere when she added, "Don't worry, Sissy. I'll pay for both of us, and you too, Doris. I wouldn't want to go alone, and my children wouldn't be interested in going with me, nor would I want them to. We have completely different ideas about what is fun and interesting. No, I'd rather have you two with me."

From there, the conversation went toward which place would be most interesting to visit, and we decided that Ireland would be the destination for our mythical trip. "This reminds me," Miss Boo said. "I have a jigsaw puzzle of leprechauns. Would you two be interested in working it, since we're confined to this house? Well, Doris, you aren't, but Sissy and I are."

"I like jigsaw puzzles," Doris Benton said. "I haven't worked one in ages."

"Me too," I said.

"I think it's in the shelves in the library," Miss Boo said. "I'll go find it."

When you think about a library in your home, you imagine ones like in the movies, with a fireplace, leather furniture, and bookshelves on three or four walls. Miss Boo's isn't that big and grand, but it's more than most houses have, and it's more a library than the one at Briarwood, which has only one wall of shelves and few books on them. Miss Boo's library is about the size of a smallish bedroom with two walls of shelves packed full of reading material. Miss Boo has told me I can borrow books at any time I want. She has quite a selection, both fiction and nonfiction. I guess that anytime something catches her attention, she buys a book about it, so now she has volumes about lots of subjects. She also has fiction books by some of her favorite authors, all of them old-school, like Daphne du Maurier, Elizabeth Goudge, and Edna Ferber, and they have become favorites of mine as well. Side by side with the famous authors of the past were recently added novels by the now famous LaRue

Saint Pierre, who couldn't hold a candle to the novelists who shared the shelf.

There wasn't much furniture in her library, just an elegant mahogany desk with an accompanying chair, and a comfy armchair, just right for reading all those volumes.

"Let's spread this out on the dining room table," Miss Boo said as she took a brightly colored box from the shelf and looked at it carefully, blowing imagined dust from it. We followed her back to the dining room, and the three of us spread the thousand pieces out and turned them right-side-up, the necessary start to working a puzzle, no matter what the size.

As we were sorting, Miss Boo's phone rang. First determining who was calling, she said, "Hello, Asher. Everything is copacetic here. We're going to work a jigsaw puzzle to keep us busy," After a short pause, she said, "Okay. Thanks for checking on us. Bye."

We soon settled to connecting the pieces, the edges first, then gradually adding the interior. There were so many shades of green. "You know," Miss Boo said, "working this puzzle is like solving the mystery of who killed Lorraine Coggins."

"How so, Boo?" Doris asked. "Explain yourself."

"Sometimes the jigsaw pieces look like they fit, but they don't. You try and try, but they just don't go where you think they should. When you eventually find the right spot, they fit perfectly. You just didn't see what the picture was going to be. You were looking at it wrong. When you finally see it another way, the pieces fall into place."

"Like this piece I just put in," I said. "I thought the orange was part of the copper pots in this corner." I pointed. "I kept going back and trying, over and over. But it wasn't a copper pot at all, it was a red-haired leprechaun in the upper corner."

"Exactly!" Miss Boo said. "So, what are we looking at wrong? What should we look at from a different perspective?" She propped herself on one elbow and stared off into space.

"I'll tell you what I want to look at now," Doris said. "Lunch! That Chinese food is calling my name."

"I'm with you on that," Miss Boo agreed. "Let's go eat. We can do more on this puzzle after lunch."

CHAPTER THIRTY-ONE

The food Doris Benton brought was delicious. She had ordered four different dishes plus rice and egg rolls, and we passed the boxes around the kitchen table several times before ending with fortune cookies.

"I have ice cream if anyone wants it," Miss Boo said.

"I'm full," I said.

"Me, too," Doris agreed. "Maybe later."

"Shall we go back to the puzzle or watch a movie on the television?"

"What movies do you have, Boo?" Doris asked.

"Better than that, I have several services. We have a big selection to choose from."

Just then, the front doorbell sounded throughout the house. We immediately froze in place, and Miss Boo put a finger over her lips. After a few seconds, she whispered, "Who could that be?"

"Somebody selling something?" Doris whispered.

"Maybe."

We stood there, frozen, while we thought about what to do. When the eight melodic notes came again, Miss Boo suggested, "Let's look out the living room window and see who it is." We quietly moved into the large quiet room that overlooked the front yard, and pulling the drapery back slightly, we peeked out on the entrance porch.

Miss Boo chuckled. "Trish Coggins, making a visit, complete with flowers and a bakery box."

"What should we do?" Doris queried. "Ignore her?"

"That seems unnecessarily rude," Miss Boo answered.

"But I'm sure Ash doesn't want us letting anybody in," I said.

"I'm sure he doesn't," Miss Boo agreed.

"So, what do we do?" Doris repeated.

"How about opening the door and talking to her but not letting her in?" Miss Boo suggested. "A compromise. We can take the gifts and tell her we'll be in contact in a day or two."

"That might work," Doris agreed.

I kept quiet, and when Miss Boo went to open the door, I kept several feet behind her.

"How lovely to see you again, Trish," Miss Boo said when she opened the door.

"I wanted to repay your visit," Trish said. "You and your assistant," she nodded her head in my direction, "were so kind to come and welcome me to Mount Chapel."

She was even more flamboyant than she'd been the day we'd dropped by at her home, unannounced. Her hair seemed bigger and blonder, her clothes shorter and tighter. "I brought you cookies and flowers," she said as she thrust the bouquet toward Miss Boo, who had no option other than to take them.

"That was very thoughtful of you, Trish, and I'm sorry that I can't ask you in, but I'm expecting. . . ." At that point she fizzled out, unable to quickly come up with who the imaginary visitor might be.

As Trish pushed the bakery box forward, she took a step into the house. Miss Boo automatically stepped back to avoid a push in that direction and holding the flowers in one hand, took the box in the other.

Trish's face still displayed the same expression, but her simpering tone of voice changed. Her right hand went into the purse she had slung over her shoulder and pulled out a gun. A small but deadly gun. "I'm afraid I have to insist," she said. I was standing about five feet farther back in the entrance hall, and she waved it toward me as well. "You too, Sissy or Cecelia or whoever you are. You aren't an assistant or whatever you're supposed to be. You're a reporter for the newspaper."

Just then, Miss Boo's phone, which was in her pocket, played the few notes that signaled a call. "Don't answer that," Trish commanded.

She took several steps into the room and used the hand not holding the gun to give the door a shove closed. "Did you think I wouldn't find out who you were? You weren't being good neighbors, welcoming me to Mount Chapel. That was just a ruse, a cover-up for why you were really there." Her voice got louder, more strident with each step. "I don't know why you two busybodies are sticking your nose into matters that don't concern you. You," she waved the gun in my direction, "you found LaRue Saint Pierre's—or I should say—Lorraine Coggins's body, and you wrote about it for the newspaper. But you've been spending so much time running around with your buddy here that you supposedly got fired. Or is that just a story?

"Maybe, since you aren't at the *News* office every day," she gestured with the gun again, "you might not have heard the latest happenings around town. There have been several break-ins lately. Robberies in affluent neighborhoods. Somebody even broke into my house, among others. While Milton was in New York and I was shopping, I came home and found the evidence and called the police, but they didn't catch whoever did it, and I never recovered my property.

"Thank heavens nobody has been hurt up until now. Unfortunately, you two won't be so lucky. You've been traveling so much lately, the robber didn't expect to find anyone home, you see. And you are, after all, the richest person in Mount Chapel. There must be tons of valuable things in your home, ripe for the taking." She waved the pistol around as she spoke.

Miss Boo's phone had stopped ringing but now mine started.

"Answer it," Trish commanded. "Say that everything is fine. If whoever it is called earlier, say that you were in the bathroom. Understand?"

I nodded.

"Any attempt to send a message will get your friend killed sooner rather than later, so be careful, *capiche*?" I nodded again.

"Hello." I felt like my voice wobbled, but I tried to hold it steady. On the other end, Asher's voice sounded concerned.

"I just tried Granny Boo's phone, and she didn't answer. Are you okay?"

"Sure," I answered. "We're okay."

There was a pause before he asked, "What was that password? Copacetic? Is everything copacetic?"

I took a deep breath before answering. "No. Absolutely not. Everything is fine."

"We'll be right there," he said and was gone.

"Good job," Trish said. "That'll keep you alive a bit longer."

"I don't see why you're doing this," I replied.

"Because you'd never stop," she answered. "You'd keep on poking and prodding and sticking your noses into places where you don't belong."

"Trish, may I ask a question?" Miss Boo said.

Trish didn't answer but looked at her with raised eyebrows. Taking this as a "yes", Miss Boo continued. "Why? Why kill Lorraine? For that matter, why kill us?"

"Like I said, because you would never leave it alone."

"What, Trish? Leave what alone?"

"Lorraine's death."

"At least, can you tell us why she died? What was she doing that was the cause of her death?"

"She was profiting from the work of someone else. She claimed credit for something she didn't do. She didn't write all those books. She didn't write even one of them."

"I understand, Trish. I really do," Miss Boo said in a soothing tone of voice. "I know Milton wrote the books. But he and Lorraine came to an agreement about that a long time ago. People just don't buy romance books written by a man, and Lorraine agreed to be the face of LaRue Saint Pierre for a share of the money, while Milton remained anonymous."

"She could be LaRue Saint Pierre forever," Trish said, "but Milton ought to have gotten the money for writing them. She could have the publicity, the magazine write-ups, and the interviews. All the fame could have been hers. My husband tried to talk to her about it, but she refused to do what he wanted. She said she never would and told him to get out of her home and never come back. A man can just take so much before he snaps."

Larry's growl was so soft that it was almost unheard. It was hard to keep from averting my eyes in his direction, but she was waving the gun and that kept my attention on her, rather than on the dog, who was stealthily creeping toward her.

"You two really should've just minded your own business instead of sticking your nose into places it didn't belong," she said. She raised the barrel of the gun slightly, as if she was taking aim at Miss Boo.

That's when Larry made his move. With a loud snarl, he clamped onto her ankle and didn't let go. Trish screamed, and the louder she shrieked, the harder he bit, his growls growing in proportion. You would've thought he was battling a bear, at the very least. The gun was waving wildly, and when it went off, the hanging crystals in the chandelier jingled and shards of glass fell to the floor.

"Hands up! Drop your gun!" The voice was Asher's, and it was echoed by similar voices from both the front and the back of the house. Suddenly, the house was filled with policemen, all pointing guns at Trish, who continued to scream.

Asher lunged forward and grabbed her arm, while another officer took the gun from her hand. Trish continued to fill the air with screams.

"Stop, Larry! Stop," Ash commanded, and after one more ferocious growl, Larry released his prey and backed up. He sat down and proudly looked up at Asher. He looked as if he was expecting something. I didn't know if he wanted a treat or a compliment.

After placing her in handcuffs, the police hustled Trish off. I heard one of them begin the famous statement that everyone who watches cop shows on TV is familiar with, while Asher stayed behind and enfolded his grandmother in a gigantic hug. He held her for long seconds then released her and moved to me. His arms around me felt so good. Like safety. Like I wasn't going to die. At least that night.

CHAPTER THIRTY-TWO
ONE WEEK LATER

As the crowd circulated throughout Miss Boo's house, Ash said, "I knew Granny Boo ought to have had this shindig at the country club."

"It was just intended to be for family and a few friends," I answered.

"Yeah, but a few friends to my grandmother is still a crowd."

Just then, Asher's mother approached us. She slipped her arm through his as she smiled at me. "Sissy, I don't know whether to be happy you and Mother are friends or not. You either are part of her getting into dangerous situations or a help in getting her out of them."

"I think Gran is perfectly capable of getting herself into danger all by herself," Ash said. "I'm not happy that Sissy gets in trouble along with her, but at least she's there to help rein her in." He grinned at me. "Or else be in trouble with her."

"True. Mother was always getting herself into hard spots before she ever met Sissy." The tall, sophisticated woman said. "How are you adjusting to living in small-town southern Mississippi?" she asked me.

"Just fine," I answered. "I was raised in small-town northern Mississippi, after all, and there's not much difference."

"I imagine not," she said. "I'd forgotten where you moved here from." She took a step closer and lowered her voice. Looking across the room where Gene Hoskins was deep in conversation with the Chief of Police, she said, "I heard that you were fired from your job at the *News*. Soon I'm going to be announcing my run for public office, and I'm going to need somebody to organize and coordinate the volunteers, put out press releases and all that. Would you be interested in the job? It would be a paid position."

"Actually," I replied, "my firing was a made-up deal. I wasn't really fired. It was all for show."

"Oh?"

"Primarily it was to keep any possible attack on me out of the office. If I no longer worked there, anybody who wanted to kill me because I might be able to identify the man with Trish Coggins wouldn't look for me there."

"We knew that Gran had seen him at the car agency and could recognize him," Ash told his mother. "But at that point, we didn't know that Sissy had seen him as well. If we had known that earlier, we would have sent Sissy out of town as well."

"I'm back at work now," I said. "I'm writing an article praising Larry for helping to save us. If not for him, Trish might have shot us both before help could get there."

"I have something I couldn't talk about earlier," Ash said, "and it's an even better story."

"Can you talk about it now?" I asked. "More than that, can I write about it now?"

"Yes, I can and you can. It's about the same mysterious man seen with Trish. The one in the lineup."

"Her brother?"

"The man she said was her brother," Ash said, grinning that lopsided grin of his.

"You mean he wasn't?"

"He wasn't her brother, he was her husband."

My mouth fell open, but words were stuck and wouldn't come out.

"If you'll excuse me," Asher's mother said, appearing to have lost interest in the subject. "I need to go speak with Gene Hoskins." She released Ash's arm and walked away.

"What do you mean, husband? Isn't she married to Milton Coggins?"

"Not legally," he responded. "She was already married when they went through some sort of scam ceremony."

"You're going to have to explain that," I said.

"It's like this: when Milton went to Vegas with his sister, he sort of went wild. Lorraine, under the name of LaRue Saint Pierre, was giving interviews and doing photo shoots to promote the book that was being released at the time. One that she supposedly had written. Of course, now we know what we didn't back then, that Milton was the author of all the books credited to LaRue Saint Pierre.

"Once Milton got to Vegas, he started drinking and playing poker and blackjack, feeding money into the slots, basically oozing money, and when Trish and her husband saw him, they saw a mark, an opportunity just waiting for them. They did a little research and found out how much money the LaRue Saint Pierre books brought in, so they set their sights on Milton Coggins.

"He was an easy target. He'd never had the attention of a woman before, at least one like Trish. She and her husband cooked up a scheme of a fake marriage, and Milton was too drunk, as well as besotted at the attention of such a glamourous woman, to recognize what was happening. If you think about it, Trish appeared to be the embodiment of the women he wrote about in all those LaRue Saint Pierre books. Beautiful and flashy with a heart of gold. And now he had just such a woman supposedly in love with him. They got an accomplice to play the part of a minister, borrowed a wedding chapel, came up with a fake marriage license, and before you know it, Milton and Trish were married—but not legally. At the time, they didn't know that Milton was the real author of the books attributed to LaRue Saint Pierre. They just knew he had money to spend, plenty of it. They found out later that he was the writer behind the pen name."

"It seems impossible that they could pull off such an elaborate scheme without being found out," I said.

"They made sure Milton was kept inebriated most of the time. He was indulged and fed praise and compliments and didn't truly sober up until they were back here in Mount Chapel, and supposedly married.

"Lorraine had already bought Briarwood and was in the midst of remodeling it. When she was growing up here, Briarwood was the epitome of success. The castle on the hill, so to speak. It was the symbol of everything the Coggins family never had. Wealth and fame and everything that went along with it.

"Before that, the plan had been to make Milton pay for getting a fake divorce from the scam marriage, but when they got here, Trish and her actual husband revised their strategy. Why not stay married to Milton for a while and see what else they could profit from?

"Lorraine, as LaRue, wouldn't put up with another glitzy character in her brother's life to compete with her for being the flashy one, the woman everybody looked at. She took one look at Milton's bride and threw a fit, so Trish temporarily altered her appearance. She became a dowdy wife, leaving LaRue as the only glamourous woman in Milton's life. Neither woman was happy in the situation, but they lived with it. After Lorraine's death, after the funeral, Trish reverted to her old appearance."

"So how did all that lead to murder?" I asked.

"Trish and her husband decided they wanted a bigger share of the take. By then, Briarwood was fully remodeled and furnished in LaRue style—gaudy and impressive as befitting the author of the popular books. LaRue had even showed off the secret passageways and suggested that Milton write a book using them in the plot. One time when Lorraine wasn't home, Milton had proudly shown them to Trish, telling her that his sister had tasked him with writing a book that used them as a plot device. Unbeknownst to him, Trish had then shown them to her real husband, who, by that point, was alternating spending time in Vegas and here in Mount Chapel."

"It seems to me that murdering Lorraine was like killing the goose that laid the golden egg," I speculated.

"You would think so," Ash agreed. "And probably it was a flash of temper that caused it. I don't think it happened on purpose."

"Which one of them pulled the trigger? Trish or her husband?"

"That's the problem. Each of them says the other one did it. They're happy to throw the other one to the wolves, as long as they come out of it as the innocent party. We have both of them in lockup." Ash shook his head. "They'll probably both be charged with murder."

"What about Milton?" I asked.

"After being totally blindsided by all this, he's stunned by the developments. I don't think I've ever seen or imagined such a naïve man. Although it might change, at this point there are no plans to charge him with any crime. He's a victim in all this," Ash said. "Additionally, he's totally sick and tired of writing the romance books that were credited to his sister. Although Trish and her real husband came up with the idea of her taking up the persona of an author of a series of successful romance books, that was never in the cards. On his last trip to talk with the publisher in person, he struck a deal to begin writing in his own name. He's going to produce a series of 'who-done-its' with a male detective as the main character. With all the writing experience he has, even if it's from a female point of view, he ought to do well."

"Especially when all this murder story comes out," I said. "Everybody and their brother will want to read whatever he writes."

"Exactly," Ash agreed. "He'll be starting with a fan base before the first book is even written."

Just then, Miss Boo walked up, Gene Hoskins at her elbow.

"Sissy, I hope you're ready to get back to writing for the *News*," Gene said. "You have some interesting columns to write."

"I've been working on some things already," I answered.

"Great! I can't wait to read them," he said.

"Oh, Gene." Miss Boo said. "I wanted to take Sissy to Memphis with me. She needs a vacation from all this murder talk."

"Memphis? What's in Memphis?" he asked.

"Shopping!" Miss Boo said. "And the pyramid."

"The Peabody Ducks," I said. "And the zoo."

"And Sissy hasn't had any vacation time since she started working at the *News*," Miss Boo added.

"This is not the time to take time off," Gene grumbled. "Too many things are happening, and Sissy is just the person to write about them."

I was quick to speak for the chance to further become a reporter rather than a receptionist. "And I'll be glad to write about them. I have lots of ideas for articles."

"Well, I'll think about it," my boss mumbled. "The time off to go to Memphis, that is. It's a yes for writing more."

"That would be wise, Gene," Miss Boo said. "You certainly don't want her to write for some other paper. Like the *Commercial Appeal*, for instance."

"Are you threatening me, Boo?"

"Yes," Miss Boo said, "I am."

Ash slipped his hand around my arm and gently urged me away from the older couple, whose conversation was rapidly evolving into a squabble about newspapers and readership and what readers were interested in.

"I think," Asher said, his mouth close to my ear as his voice dropped to just over a whisper, "that if you plan a trip to Memphis, I need to go along to keep you safe."

"Oh? Safe from what?"

"The Peabody Ducks," he said, his breath on my skin giving me goosebumps. "I hear they attack unsuspecting guests. I need to be there to protect you."

I'm still thinking about that. He might be right. It might be better to keep Asher Donovan close by at all times. Just to be safe, you know.

ABOUT THE AUTHOR

Nancy Smith Gibson has been a voracious reader from an early age, but didn't start writing until she had an empty nest—if you can call it empty when she shares it with a rescue dog and two rescue cats. She is the mother of four, grandmother of four, and great-grand of two.

Her professional years were spent as a "number please" and long distance telephone operator and supervisor, a census supervisor for various government surveys, and in real estate sales. For some years, she also produced crafts for sales at arts and crafts fairs. The people she met and situations she encountered provide rich fodder for stories.

She is also active in genealogy research, tracing her family roots back several generations.

She writes contemporary and historical "sweet" romances, often including mystery and suspense, as well as magical realism and not-so-real witches.

Made in the USA
Columbia, SC
25 July 2023